Nothing will ever be the same again for Lila . . .

Lila pressed her hot face longingly against the glass. The moonlit night outside looked so cool— so free and empty!

And how hot, how stifling it was inside this tiny, cramped room. She could hardly *breathe* in here! And her skin felt so strange, so prickling, as though tiny insects were crawling under it. . . .

Must get outside.

Lila began to whimper. The wound on her leg was a maddening pulse now. *Out, out, out, out, out,* it clamored in her veins.

CHILDREN OF THE NIGHT

DARK DREAMS

ANN HODGMAN

PUFFIN BOOKS

Grateful acknowledgment is made for permission to reprint "Night-Piece," by Raymond R. Patterson. Published in *Why Am I Grown So Cold?*, ed. Myra Cohn Livingston (Atheneum, 1982).

For Matt, of course
And, of course, for Tisha

PUFFIN BOOKS
Published by the Penguin Group
Penguin Books USA Inc., 375 Hudson Street, New York, New York 10014, U.S.A.
Penguin Books Ltd, 27 Wrights Lane, London W8 5TZ, England
Penguin Books Australia Ltd, Ringwood, Victoria, Australia
Penguin Books Canada Ltd, 10 Alcorn Avenue, Toronto, Ontario, Canada M4V 3B2
Penguin Books (N.Z.) Ltd, 182–190 Wairau Road, Auckland 10, New Zealand

Penguin Books Ltd, Registered Offices: Harmondsworth, Middlesex, England

First published in the United States of America by Puffin Books,
a division of Penguin Books USA Inc., 1993

1 3 5 7 9 10 8 6 4 2

Copyright © Ann Hodgman, 1993
All rights reserved

Library of Congress Cataloging-in-Publication Data

Hodgman, Ann.
Dark dreams / Ann Hodgman.
p.   cm.—(Children of the night; #1) (Puffin high flyer)
Summary: Sixteen-year-old Lila, a beautiful and popular student,
finds her perfect life shattered by her transformation into a
werewolf.
ISBN 0-14-036374-2.
[1. Werewolves—Fiction. 2. Supernatural—Fiction. 3. Horror—
Fiction.] I. Title. II. Series. III. Series: Puffin high flyer.
PZ7.H6648Dar 1993   93-15039   [Fic]—dc20   CIP
AC

Printed in the United States of America
Set in New Baskerville
High-Flyer™ is a trademark of Puffin Books, a division of Penguin Books USA Inc.

I do not sleep at night.
Rain does not lull me, and the withered wind
Is always out of tune, when there is wind
Or moon enough for light.

The sounds, up from the street,
Fall back again, unclaimed: The dispossessed
Call out with longing to the dispossessed.
The sounds repeat, repeat . . .

But never call my name;
Though I have heard the footsteps mount the stair,
The steady tread that echoed down the stair—
And trembled just the same . . .

As if someone had come
But could not find me, passing by my room,
And did not know I waited in my room,
Lonely, sleepless and dumb.

    —Raymond R. Patterson, from "Night-Piece"

PROLOGUE

In the shadow behind the ruined cathedral of Aubigny, a wolf is waiting.

Winters here are wicked. The cold is so bitter it hurts to breathe, so cruel that cobblestones shatter and birds, flying, freeze and fall lifeless to earth. Knife-sharp icicles glitter perilously from the eaves of the ancient stone houses, and the snow is packed as smooth and hard as glass.

The sun set five hours ago. Now the streets of this tiny town lie petrified under the full moon's pitiless blue stare. The wolf crouches silently in the shadows.

He is used to waiting.

Three ancient stone houses face the cathedral's cobbled courtyard. On some evenings, the lights in the houses are warm and bright. Tonight, though, only a window or two is lit, and the houses are silent. A woman stops before a window the ice has sealed shut. She touches the glass with a forefinger, shivers, and pulls away from the window.

The wolf whines quietly. The centuries he has spent roaming the French countryside in search of prey have taught him patience, but he is terribly hungry.

Suddenly a door creaks open in the middle house. A child's blonde head peers cautiously into the darkness.

A child. A little girl, maybe three years old. A child can't move very fast. A child might make a mistake.

The girl opens the heavy door a little wider and slips out of the house, shivering in her pink nightgown.

The door bangs shut behind her.

The wolf is on his feet now. Silent as a cat, he too steps forward, to the very edge of the shadow falling from the cathedral. His mouth is watering. He runs a tongue over his pointed teeth.

"Oh, *there* you are!" says the little girl as she spies

her doll at the foot of the steps. Clutching the icy iron railing gingerly, she pads down the steep steps toward her baby.

The wolf tenses to spring.

Is there no one who can protect this child?

Her soft pink hand reaches down for the doll.

Snarling, the wolf vaults across the narrow street and hurls himself at her.

With a thin scream, the child drops her doll and tries to pull out of his way. But the steps are too steep for her chubby legs. She manages to scramble up only one of them before the wolf, growling horribly, is upon her. His teeth are ravenous for her throat. . . .

At just that moment, the door swings open. "No!" a woman shrieks in terror. "My God, *no!*" Faster than a heartbeat, she springs down the steps and grabs her daughter's arm. The wolf's claws rake across the little girl's leg, but he never gets the chance to bite. In an instant mother and child are back inside. The door slams behind them, and the wolf streaks back into the shadows.

He has no time to regret his loss. He must escape

the town quickly. He will have to find his prey somewhere else tonight.

Forgotten once again, the doll rolls off the last step and lies facedown in the snow.

CHAPTER 1

I don't belong here.

Sixteen-year-old Lila Crawford sighed as she stared around the crowded cafeteria at Pelham High School. It was the usual drab, noisy sty, but at that moment she felt as though she'd never noticed before how truly horrible it was. Frayed posters hanging crooked and defaced on the dingy walls, some teacher's hopeless attempt to cheer things up. Linoleum floor crusted with crumbs and muddy sneaker-prints and sticky with soda spills. The smell of dirty steam that has perfumed every school cafeteria since schools began. And rising above everything else, the feverish pitch of two hundred students with exactly eighteen minutes to relax before the afternoon bell goes off.

Yes, it was a familiar scene. But today, somehow,

watching it all gave Lila the sense that she had somehow wandered into the wrong life by mistake.

"Who died, Lila?" her best friend Samantha Bardel suddenly said, breaking into Lila's reverie. Samantha was sitting next to Lila at the lunch table; their other best friend, Marci Zwick, was sitting across from them. As usual, Samantha's lunch consisted of a donut and a bag of chips. Lila didn't recall ever seeing her take a bite of real food. Marci, who never ate where anyone could see her, was lunching solely on a diet soda. "What're you thinking about?" Samantha went on.

Lila nodded at the scene in front of them. "I'm just sick of this place, I guess," she said. "It gets a little disgusting, don't you think?"

Marci turned and scanned the room. "Doesn't look so bad to me," she said acidly. "Just a bunch of people eating their lunch, that's all. Do you want everyone sitting around with their hands folded?"

"No, but . . ."

Lila didn't bother finishing the sentence. She was suddenly afraid she sounded like a goody-goody. After all, what did she have to complain about? It wasn't as if this cafeteria was her major source of excitement. The bulk of the kids sitting around her couldn't possibly have as much fun as she did. Plenty of them probably didn't have any friends, while she, Lila, had too many to keep track of. *In fact,* she thought, trying to cheer herself up, *it's probably safe to say that everyone in this cafeteria would be my friend if they got the chance (even that poor Nancy Bailey in the corner, who keeps all those tropical fish in her bedroom).* And how many people could say that? Not even Samantha and Marci were as popular, though they certainly came close.

"You know who *I* think's disgusting," Samantha said, "that moron, Todd Hecht." She grimaced disdainfully at a tall, gangling boy sitting alone at a table across the room from them. He was reading a book intently, trying to look as though he didn't notice the straws the guys at the next table were blowing his way. "Doesn't he make you totally *gag?*"

Lila shrugged. "Not really. He's not that bad, actually. He's in my algebra class."

"Oh, come on," said Marci. "He's a complete parasite."

"You don't even know him," Lila retorted. "How can you—"

Samantha snorted. "It's easy for you to talk, Lila. *You're* only going out with the cutest guy in the whole school. You can *afford* to be nice about the losers the rest of us are stuck with."

"I'm not being nice!" Lila protested. "I'm just telling the truth! Todd doesn't make me gag, okay? I'm not saying I'd go out with him."

"That's exactly what I mean," Samantha cut in.

"I'm just saying he doesn't make me gag. So stop looking at me like I'm crazy."

Now Marci spoke up again. "You know Lila's always sticking up for people," she drawled, stabbing her straw venomously into her soda can. "She's not satisfied just being the prettiest girl in the junior class and having the best boyfriend and all. She wants to be the *nicest* person in the school, too. She thinks she's Mother Theresa or something."

"I do not!" Lila objected. "I just don't feel like spending every single lunch period making fun of people! Can't we talk about something else for a change besides who we hate?"

Marci gave an elaborate sigh. "O-*kay*. Let's talk about this delicious cafeteria food. Then we can talk about the fascinating classes we're taking. And *then* maybe we can get into something *really* worthwhile, like the weather or poor people or something. Thank you for improving our lunchtime conversation, Lila."

Lila didn't bother answering. *It's not worth it,* she thought wearily. *I'm too tired to argue with them today.*

Marci Zwick was right about one thing, anyway. Lila *was* the—well, not the prettiest girl in the school, maybe, but one of them. Auburn hair, huge, liquid amber eyes, the perfect face and body—Lila couldn't think of a time she hadn't found her own appearance tremendously reassuring. Her two best friends looked pretty good, too. Samantha was a classic blue-eyed blonde. "Like something from a shampoo ad," Lila always teased her. And Marci had a cloud of dark-brown ringlets and huge black eyes. The three girls made such a perfect combination that sometimes Lila wondered uneasily whether that was the reason they were such good friends.

But naturally she didn't say anything about that particular suspicion to Samantha and Marci. It certainly wasn't the kind of thing you talked about, even to your best friends. Besides, the three girls' personalities were complementary in the same way. Marci was the edgy, sophisticated one, Samantha was the nice, enthusiastic one (even though sometimes she did remind Lila of an overeager puppy), and Lila—Lila fell somewhere in between. Sometimes Marci irritated her, sometimes Samantha exhausted her, but for the most part the three of them got along very well.

What am I doing here?

Lila glanced up, startled. It had been her own voice she'd heard. Had she spoken out loud? It seemed that she hadn't. At least, neither Marci nor Samantha seemed to have noticed anything.

"Are you guys going to the game after school?" Samantha asked in a smoothing-things-over voice. Pelham's varsity football team had started off the season with five straight wins, three of them upsets, and almost the whole school had started showing up at games.

"Of course she's going to be there," said Marci. "She's got to cheer for Corey. Being the girlfriend of the great Corey Ryan is a full-time job."

Lila smiled weakly. "I have to confess, sometimes

I wish that Corey didn't even play football. It gets a little monotonous watching him win every single game. But yes, I'll probably be there. If I stop feeling so tired, that is. What I'd really like to do is go home and take a nap."

"You *do* look terrible," Marci said helpfully. "All pale and dragged out. Are you feeling all right?"

Lila shook her head. "I think I must be coming down with something. My whole body feels as though I've been hit by a truck. My head, my joints, my leg."

"Your *leg?*" Samantha interrupted. "What did you do to your leg?"

Lila reached down to rub the spot on her calf that had been throbbing on and off all day. "I must have banged it or something," she said. "I've had this little scar there since I was a baby, but for some reason it's really bothering me today."

She glanced down at her leg as she spoke—and gasped.

The scar on her right calf was so tiny, three white, threadlike lines just half an inch long, that Lila had never paid much attention to it. In fact, she didn't even know how she'd gotten it. Now, though, the scar was an inflamed red, and it had swelled angrily as though it were infected.

"Yuck!" Samantha shuddered as she glanced down at Lila's leg too. "What happened to you? That looks horrible!"

"I . . . I don't know. But no wonder it's been bothering me."

"You'd better have the nurse take a look at it," Samantha advised. "Maybe you've got some kind of weird bug bite or something."

"Some kind of weird food poisoning, more likely," Marci said dryly. "That's what this place will do to you."

Lila laughed politely. *How many cafeteria jokes have I heard since first grade?* she wondered. *Hundreds? Thousands?* These days she could barely muster up a smile when she heard one. And how many more would she have to suffer through before she finished high school and college?

Clear but distant, like the chime of a muted bell, she seemed to hear her own voice again.

I've got to get out of here, it was telling her.

But there was no place to go.

Pelham won the football game 31-10, and Lila was there to see it—as well as she *could* see anything through eyes that were three-quarters closed. At one point she felt so woozy that she almost toppled off the bleachers, but Samantha gave her a warning pinch before she could embarrass herself.

"Wake *up!*" Samantha hissed into Lila's ear. "Don't you *care* about this game?"

Not exactly.

Still, Lila forced herself to sit up straight. What would Corey think if he looked up into the stands and caught her dozing off? What kind of supportive girlfriend would *that* make her?

Every high school has a boy like Corey Ryan—a star, a golden child, the one whose name all the parents know. You can pick out a boy like this in the first grade and track him all the way through school, and he'll never miss a step. He's always the only ninth-grader on the varsity team. He's always the one who gets to escort the governor around when she visits the school. He's the one who never does anything wrong but never alienates people, either. He's always polite, even to people who don't matter. He makes the all-state team and wins the Good Citizenship award and marches off to a nice college without ever wavering. You can't not like someone like Corey Ryan.

When she'd first started going out with Corey, Lila had spent most of her waking time marveling at her good luck. She'd gone out with enough boys to know that the All-American types could be pretty horrible. "Either they're totally in love with themselves and totally horrible to everyone who doesn't like sports or they act as though they're *campaigning* for something all the time," she had once complained to Samantha.

But Corey . . . Corey got along with everyone. He couldn't have been mean or selfish. It wouldn't have occurred to him. He was too happy for that—too happy, in a world where the sun had always shone on him, to bother finding fault with other people. *And he's mine! I got him!* Lila kept telling herself jubilantly.

But today, for some reason, Lila didn't feel much of anything when Corey loped across the field toward her after the game.

"Hey, babe!" He was grinning happily and shaking back the long blond hair that always got in his eyes. (The coach hated Corey's hair, but Corey played so well that he never had any excuse for making him cut it.) "How'd we do?"

"You know the answer to that," Lila said with a smile, leaning down from her seat to kiss him. His face was as flushed and cheerful as a one-year-old's, she thought.

Corey reached up and ruffled her hair as Samantha and Marci melted discreetly out of sight. "Want to, you know, take a walk later, or something?" he asked. "After I've changed?"

"Um—well, actually, Corey . . ."

Lila hesitated. Her leg was hurting more than ever, and her head was starting to really throb. All she wanted to do was go home and fall into bed. "I'm kind of tired," she said reluctantly.

Corey's face fell as though she'd slapped him. "But we just won the game!" he said in a bewildered voice.

"So what do you want? A *reward*?" Lila snapped before she could stop herself. Then she clapped her hand over her mouth.

"Oh, Corey, I'm sorry," she said in horror. "I didn't mean that at *all*. I don't know what's the matter with me today."

"That's okay, babe," Corey said slowly. "If you're not feeling well . . ."

But now Lila couldn't stand to see him looking so disappointed. "I'm sure there's nothing wrong with me that some time with you wouldn't cure," she said quickly. "Really, Corey. I mean it." She shook a teasing forefinger at him. "You go and get unsweaty, now. I'll meet you in front of the school."

Like magic the grin reappeared on Corey's face. "Sounds good," he said.

Tired as she was, Lila couldn't help smiling back. "It doesn't take much to make *you* happy," she said.

Corey reached up, pulled her down to him, and kissed her again. "Don't sell yourself short," he whispered.

Half an hour later the two of them were strolling through the woods that bordered the reservoir near Lila's neighborhood. This was one of Lila's favorite spots. The woods themselves were beautiful—a lacy, dark-green space made hushed and mysterious by the overhanging branches of hundreds of hemlock trees. The path downhill led to a rocky brook punctuated with little waterfalls. The path uphill led to the town reservoir, which was ringed with a stone wall and a miniature stone gatehouse with a pointed slate roof. Lila and Corey had taken the reservoir path this time, and now they were leaning their elbows on the stone wall and gazing into the quiet depths below.

"I used to think that gatehouse was enchanted when I was little," Lila mused, looking over at the tiny building. "I wonder what it's used for?"

"Probably fuseboxes or something." Corey didn't sound especially interested. "Whatever kind of stuff you need to run a reservoir."

"*Fuseboxes?*" Lila couldn't help laughing. "Corey, you are the *most* unromantic person I've ever met."

The minute the words were out, she wished she hadn't said them. *Now Corey will feel as though he has to prove I'm wrong,* she thought in a sudden panic, *and I just can't stand to have him touch me today. I shouldn't have—*

But it was too late. "Unromantic, huh?" Corey said, putting an arm around Lila's shoulders and pulling her closer to him. "I hate to argue with you, but *I* think I'm a *very* romantic guy." He kissed Lila gently on the nose. His eyes were almost painfully blue as they gazed down at her. "What do you think?"

For the first time in her life Lila fought a wild, unreasoning urge to pull out of his arms. "I—of course you are," she stammered, feeling panic rise in her like nausea. "But it—it's kind of getting late, Corey. We should be—"

"It's not *that* late," Corey said huskily. "We've still got some time." His arms tightened around Lila, and his mouth reached for hers.

Get me out of here! For a terrible moment, Lila thought again she'd spoken aloud. *But I couldn't have,* she thought desperately. *Corey's still aiming at me.*

What was the matter with her? On other days, she couldn't wait to get Corey all to herself! So why was she so . . . repulsed by him all of a sudden?

Now he was kissing her, and something deep inside her was choking, suffocating at this closeness. But Lila shut her eyes, forcing herself to relax and kiss Corey back. Her temples were throbbing so painfully she could hardly stand up, but that wasn't Corey's fault. It would hurt his feelings if she didn't respond. After all, she *loved* him, didn't she?

Yes, she thought desperately, *but not now. I can't stand this. I've got to be alone—*

"I love you so much, babe," Corey was murmuring as he kissed her neck. "So much more than I ever thought I could. You know that, don't you?"

"It doesn't make any difference," Lila heard herself saying flatly.

And suddenly she realized that this time she *had* spoken out loud.

"What?" Corey took a step backward, staring baffled at her. "What did you say?"

"I—nothing." Lila was gasping for breath. "It was . . ."

There was nothing she could say to him. There was no way she could stand to be near him for even one more second.

"Corey, I've got to go," Lila said, wrenching herself out of his arms. "I'm sorry, but I've got to go home right now."

And before Corey could say a word to stop her, she was dashing down the hill and stumbling through the woods toward home.

Corey speaks

I swear it's not anything I did to her. She just . . . changed all of a sudden. One minute she was like she'd always been, and the next . . .

I'm not superstitious or anything. Maybe superstitious isn't the word I want, anyway. What I mean is, I don't believe in ghosts or exorcism or anything like that.

But Lila was . . . I guess possessed *is the only word. She was taken over by something when we were out in the woods that day. And I never saw the real Lila—my Lila—again. She was another person after that. I know it sounds impossible, but I'm telling the truth. After that day she looked the same as always, but she never came back to me.*

I swear it wasn't anything I did. I . . . I hope it wasn't, anyway. God, I miss her so much. I hope she's all right, wherever she is. I hope she knows I'd do anything to help her—if she'd only come back.

CHAPTER 2

"Why did I do it?" Lila moaned aloud. She rocked feverishly back and forth on her bed, pressing a cool washcloth to her throbbing forehead and wishing it would help at least a little. "Poor Corey! How could I have been such a witch?"

It was nine o'clock at night. A full moon was streaming through Lila's bedroom window, and in its unforgiving light she was twitching with pain. Physical pain from whatever it was that was making her feel so sick, and mental pain from the way she had treated Corey that afternoon.

You're overreacting, she told herself. *You didn't say anything that bad, really.* What was really upsetting her, she knew, was that what she'd said to Corey had reflected only a fraction of her alienation from him. Had Corey guessed that there was more behind her words?

"He's probably furious at me," she whispered to herself. "How could I say that? I acted like someone I don't even know!"

And why on earth had she said what she'd said to him—*or* felt it, for that matter? Lila winced, remembering her words and the look on Corey's face when he'd heard them.

There are some things you have a little trouble taking back, she thought bitterly, *and what I said to Corey isn't exactly going to be easy to explain away. I wouldn't be surprised if he never speaks to me again.*

But would she care?

The thought flickered into Lila's mind for the briefest instant before she tossed it away indignantly. Of *course* she would care. She'd never forgive herself. If Corey gave up on her, it would be—

Wouldn't it actually be a relief? some devil inside her asked again.

"No, no!" Once again Lila spoke out loud. And she tried to will an image of Corey into her mind.

His smile. The blond hair that was always getting in his eyes. The way he always—

"Lila, what is going *on* in here? Are you talking to yourself?"

It was Lila's mother. She rapped angrily on the door.

"It's open," Lila called, and in a second her mother was standing at her bedside.

"What on earth are you doing in bed, honey?" Mrs. Crawford asked. As always, her tone was a blend of concern and impatience.

There *had* to have been a time when Mrs. Crawford wasn't in a hurry, but Lila couldn't remember it. For as long as she could remember, her mother had been hustling her along, nagging her to go a little faster or be a little neater or do a little better. Sickness—weakness of any kind—made Mrs. Crawford especially impatient. It slowed things down; it got in her way; it wrecked the routine. Her attitude seemed to imply that if you only had a little more self-discipline, you wouldn't get sick. Lila could almost feel her mother tensing up as she neared Lila's bed.

"Are you sick? What's going on? Is your homework done?" asked Mrs. Crawford now, staring down at her daughter. She pressed Lila's forehead so hard that Lila could feel the rings cutting into her skin. "You have a fever!" Mrs. Crawford said accusingly. "Why didn't you tell me you weren't feeling well?"

Because you would have driven me crazy worrying about how it would screw up the schedule if I was sick, Lila wanted to answer. Instead, she said, "I didn't want to bother you. With Dad away and everything." Mr. Crawford, a businessman, had been out of town at a conference for a few days. "I know you're busy."

"Bother? It's no bother!" Now her mother sounded a little irritated. "What seems to be the trouble, dear?"

"Mostly it's my leg, Mom," Lila said. Moving her leg even the slightest bit hurt terribly now. She gestured toward her calf, and her mother bent down to take a look.

Mrs. Crawford caught her breath sharply. "Lila! This is *hideous!* What have you done to it?"

Lila craned her neck down to look, and for once she could understand her mother's tone.

The sore place on her leg was festering. There was no other word for it. It had turned a sickly green-gray in the center, with yellowish streaks. And when Lila looked more closely, she could almost see the edges of the wound pulsing like some kind of living creature.

"I—I didn't do anything to it, Mom," she gasped, wrenching her eyes away from the awful sight. "It just started hurting today at school. You don't think I have some kind of blood poisoning, do you?"

Her mother frowned. "Blood poisoning? I don't think it could be that. Maybe you've just been picking at it without realizing it."

"Mom, I haven't!"

"Well, leave it alone," her mother said. "If it still hurts in the morning, I'll take you in to see the doctor." She sighed. Seeing the doctor was another break in the routine. "Now try to get some rest. It's a school day tomorrow, and if you're feeling well enough, I really think you should go."

At the doorway Mrs. Crawford paused, as if she had suddenly remembered something. "Can I get you some aspirin, Lila?" she asked.

"No thanks, Mom. Good night."

"Now, honey, whatever you do, please don't pick at that scar," was her mother's reply.

Alone in her room once more, Lila hoisted herself up painfully onto her elbows to look at her leg more closely.

To her horror, she realized the scar was starting to bubble. Tiny, evil-looking blisters, each only a pinhead in diameter, were crowding to the surface of Lila's skin as though her leg were red-hot. It was almost as if it were alive.

Lila moaned. What was she supposed to do now?

Lock your door.

"Who said that?" Lila whispered.

Lock your door, the voice repeated, and Lila realized that the commanding voice came from inside her.

Somehow it never occurred to her to do otherwise. Scrambling painfully to her feet, she hobbled awkwardly across the room and pressed the lock on her doorknob.

Go to the window.

It was another command.

Lila hobbled to the window and pressed her hot face longingly against the glass. The moonlit night outside looked so cool—so free and empty!

And how hot, how stifling it was inside this tiny, cramped room! She could hardly *breathe* in here!

And her skin felt so strange, so prickling, as though tiny insects were crawling under it. . . .

Must get outside.

Lila began to whimper. The wound on her leg was a maddening pulse now. *Out, out, out, out, out,* it clamored in her veins.

But how can I get out? she wondered, clawing desperately at the window. It wouldn't budge. Her hands didn't know how to make it work. *What is this thing?* She scratched the glass frantically, whimpering again. *Open, open, open. . . .*

Trapped in here. Must get outside. . . .

I'll die in here. . . .

Suddenly the voices in her head and the pulse in her leg and the fever coursing through her body burst into one irresistible force. The window never opened, but Lila sailed through it all the same.

Sailed through it without a cut, without even cracking the glass. Sailed through the dark air like a moth that had just burst through its chrysalis. Landed on all fours, panting gratefully as she breathed in the fragrance of the night.

And raced off into the moonlit night in the perfect form of a wolf.

The first thing the wolf notices as she races along is the absence of any valid scent. These smooth stone streets, these clipped lawns with their meaningless strips of flowers—they offer nothing interesting. Even the trees are sterile and correct.

The light is odd, too. The wolf knows it's night, and she knows there's a full moon. Yet somehow the moon can't reach her well enough here. The rows of artificial lights on the street dim its power.

The wolf slows to a doubtful trot, sniffing the asphalt anxiously. With part of her mind, she recognizes this strange, tamed setting. But isn't there something more? A wilder place, with real trees and real moonlight? She's been there before.

She raises her head and smells the air more carefully. Yes. She was right. Behind this street's bland nothingness is the tang of something more fresh, more alive. Rustling leaves. A hint of squirrel and more complicated prey. The smell of unlocked water running freely over mossy stones.

The wolf turns and dashes off. In a few minutes, she is rewarded by the sight of a dark, tangled forest on a hill. At the base of the hill is a brook. The wolf throws herself at it, the water a blessing to her parched throat. She had not known how much she needed to drink.

And now, suddenly, she realizes that she needs to eat. In fact, she is desperately, all-consumingly hungry. She is breathing hunger in and out. But although she remembers being in this forest before, she has no memory of hunting in it. Where are the animals?

She stands still to let the sounds and scents wash over her more clearly.

Old, faded skunk hits her, and raccoon, and the rankness of possum, and something like a wolf but tamer—dog, that's it. Some of the animals are asleep, she knows. Owls are awake—their smells are clearer—but she knows there's no point in thinking about an owl. She needs something that travels on the ground.

Hunger is clawing the wolf angrily now, but she forces herself to be patient and to listen. She is used to waiting.

In a few minutes she hears the faintest rustle of leaves behind her. Then a raccoon steps cautiously into the moonlight and waddles toward the brook. The wolf freezes.

The raccoon bends its head toward the water. Then, too late, it catches a whiff of the wolf's scent. It lifts its head anxiously, but before it can even think about running the wolf is upon it. One shake, and she breaks the raccoon's neck. One bite, and she tears its body in half.

What joy! Fresh raw meat, and crackling bones, and hot blood coursing onto the ground. The wolf eats ravenously, shaking with relief. When she has had all the meat she wants, she laps up the blood puddled at her feet.

Then she takes off through the woods at a rapid pace. There are still hours before the moon sets, and she wants to make the most of them.

Lila's mother speaks

I really resent these allegations. To suggest that her father or I had anything to do with Lila's disappearance is utterly ridiculous. We wouldn't dream of making her want to leave home. We were never anything but fair to our daughter. Of course we expected her to do her best. What parent doesn't? But we didn't put undue pressure on her.

She was always an emotional child, I must say. I never quite understood where she got it from. My husband and I aren't like that at all.

I suppose we'll never understand why Lila took it into her head to leave. Naturally it's very disappointing and upsetting to us. We thought we were providing everything she needed. I'm sure she'll be back once she realizes what a mistake she's made. This is still her home.

. . . What's that? Don't be silly. Naturally *I miss her. I should think that would be obvious! In a situation like this, wouldn't any* normal *parent miss her daughter?*

CHAPTER 3

Thank God it was just a dream.

Lila rubbed her burning eyes, wincing as the sun hit her face. Her mouth tasted foul, her body ached as if she'd been scaling mountains in her sleep, and she felt more tired than when she'd gone to bed. But at least it was daytime now. She could put away the visions that had tormented her throughout the night.

"Lila! Better get going, or you'll be late!" her mother called sharply up the stairs.

"I'll be right there, Mom," Lila called back. *Gee, what'd I do to my face to make it ache so much?* she wondered, passing an inquiring hand over her jaw. *Slept on it wrong, or something. Too much tension.*

With a yawn, she kicked back the covers. Then she gasped and sat bolt upright, staring down at her legs.

They were covered all over with bloody scratches—the kind of scratches you might find on someone who had spent the night running through the woods. And her feet were black with the kind of ground-in dirt you see on someone who's been pacing barefoot for hours.

I must have been . . . walking in my sleep?

But somehow Lila couldn't see herself getting past her mother if she'd left the house in the ordinary way. She glanced over at her bedroom window. It was shut, of course. She remembered closing it the night before.

Suddenly she remembered, too, the image of a wolf streaking right through the glass and landing outside the house. That had just been part of her dream, though. It hadn't really—

"What's on my face?" Lila said aloud. She'd just touched a sticky patch at one corner of her mouth, noticing as she did so that her fingernails were also torn and dirty. And her mouth was crusted with something.

She stood up and walked shakily over to the mirror above her bureau.

Her frightened reflection stared back at her.

Hair wildly snarled and snagged with twigs. Huge dark hollows under her eyes. And what was that dark, brownish stuff streaking her mouth and chin? Dried blood.

"Oh, no," Lila whispered. She staggered backward—and stepped on a small clump of fur lying on the floor.

It, too, was crusted with dried blood.

When the human brain is presented with an unbearable truth, it rushes to supply a more acceptable explanation of the facts. *I got these scratches in the woods yesterday with Corey,* Lila thought confusedly. *A cat somehow got into my room and scratched me. I bit my lip while I was sleeping. I've got some kind of fever.*

That seemed the most plausible, actually, considering how sick she felt now. But it still didn't fit.

The only explanation that *did* fit was that the dreams she'd had all night long hadn't been dreams at all.

Which would mean that she really had turned into a wolf last night. (Now she could remember exactly the dry, dead feel of the pavement under her claws as she raced for the forest.)

But of course it was impossible that she could have turned into a wolf. Which, in turn, would mean that she had spent the night roaming the woods *imagining* she was a wolf. Crouching down on her hands and knees to lap water from the brook, tearing that poor raccoon to bits with her bare hands, feeling its blood running down her throat.

Lila clapped a hand over her mouth and bolted toward the bathroom.

"That was an awfully long shower, honey," said her mother as a white-faced Lila stumbled into the kitchen. "I hope you didn't use up all the hot water. I have to shower too, you know."

"Sorry, Mom," Lila said bleakly as she sat down at the breakfast table. "I wasn't thinking, I guess."

A whole ocean of boiling water wouldn't get me clean, anyway. You can't wash this kind of thing off.

"How's your leg today?" Lila's mother asked. "Did you put a bandage on it?"

"It's about the same. Maybe a little better." *Mom, don't you see that a sore leg is the least of my problems right now? Either I'm losing my mind, or I turned into a wolf last night. Compared to that, my leg just doesn't bother me much.*

"That's nice," her mother said absently, and crossed something out on the notes she was studying. "Now, what do you want for breakfast?"

Oh, I had a—let's call it a midnight snack. I'm not hungry now. In fact, I never want to eat again.

"Just some juice," Lila mumbled. "I've got to get going or I'll be late."

"So do I." Mrs. Crawford stuffed her notes into her briefcase and stood up briskly. "I'm picking up your father at the airport after work. He'll be looking forward to seeing you, so please could you make sure you're on time for supper?"

No problem. I have nowhere else to go.

"Earth to Lila! Earth to Lila! We're sitting *here*, if you haven't noticed."

Marci and Samantha were gazing up at Lila incredulously. It was lunchtime, and the two of them had already sat down at the girls' usual cafeteria table. Lila had just passed their table while drifting, lunch tray in hand, toward an empty table in the back of the room.

Now she halted and stared vaguely down at her two best friends. She felt as if she was seeing them from a great distance. "Oh," she said after a second. "Right. Hi."

"Yes, 'hi' is what we usually say when we see people we know," said Marci patiently. "Then we sit down with them and begin to eat lunch while conversing pleasantly about the events of the day. You'll understand the ways of our planet once you've lived here longer."

Samantha giggled appreciatively, but Lila didn't even smile. "I, uh—yeah," she said. "I will. But listen, guys, I'm feeling a little tired. I mean, I've got to study. I think I'd better sit by myself today."

Samantha hastily swallowed a mouthful of potato chips. "Lila, we *always* sit together!" she said in dismay. "Are you mad about something?"

"No, no." Just speaking seemed like much too much work. "I'm just . . ."

"Just being a total alien, that's all," said Marci tartly. "I was watching you in algebra, you know. You didn't even say anything when Mr. Sherbinski called on you. He gave you the weirdest look."

Lila couldn't even *remember* algebra. A whole morning had passed in front of her, and she hadn't noticed. She had walked from class to class like a robot and then suddenly found herself in the lunchline being handed a bowl of soup. Tomato soup. It made her sick to look at it.

"What's the matter?" Marci went on. "You're *way* too out of it today. Is your family being unusually dysfunctional or something?"

"No, I just . . ." Lila felt as if the floor were wavering under her feet. Standing upright was too much work, too.

"I guess I can sit here," she finally said. "There's no reason not to."

And she pulled out a chair while Samantha and Marci stared outraged at her.

"Well!" she heard Marci snap angrily. "You *really* must be losing it if it's such a pain for you to sit with your two best friends."

I'm not losing it, Marci. I've lost it already. You try turning into a werewolf and see what kind of a mood it puts you into.

A werewolf. That was the first time Lila had let

herself think the word. All morning she'd been trying to block it out, and now it had popped into her mind unbidden.

I turned into a werewolf last night. And if I didn't, I certainly acted like one.

For no reason at all, Lila suddenly remembered the health class they'd had back in seventh grade.

A roomful of giggling, embarrassed kids. Facing them, a teacher, Miss Hempel, who was almost as embarrassed as they were. (Did they always stick the newest teachers with health class? Lila wondered. Miss Hempel hadn't been more than twenty-three or twenty-four.)

"I know it seems a little strange," Miss Hempel had said bravely. "But your bodies will be, uh, changing over the next few years"—a spurt of giggles from Samantha at that point—"and you should be prepared. Puberty is really nothing to be embarrassed about. It's all perfectly normal."

It's all perfectly normal. These changes are all perfectly normal. You'll feel a little self-conscious, of course. Maybe a little moody. But it happens to everyone.

That was what was supposed to make you feel

better—that it happened to everyone. Well, *this* certainly didn't happen to everyone.

Okay, Miss Hempel, Lila thought grimly. *I think you skipped something. Let's see how you explain the changes I'm going through.*

Another country

Full moon. Midnight. The top of a hill thousands of miles away from the forest where Lila is roaming. Frost etching the grass, bitter chill in the air.

A hooded figure uses a pointed stone to draw two circles on the hilltop, one inside the other. In the center of the inner circle, he builds a fire. Over the fire, he places a heavy cauldron.

He has spent days gathering the ingredients waiting in this cauldron. Opium. Hemlock. Parsley. Aconite. Poplar leaves. Ash. Deadly nightshade. Cowbane. Bat's blood. The last was, of course, the hardest to find. They used to use the fat of young children in this recipe, but that's even harder to manage nowadays. Oil works almost as well.

As the mixture in the cauldron begins to simmer, the hooded figure raises his arms to the moon and chants an incantation he learned centuries ago. Though his voice is cracked and old, it has eerie carrying power. The hill seems to be holding its breath, listening.

Spirits from the deep
Who never sleep,
Be kind to me, *chants the hooded figure.*

Spirits from the grave
Without a soul to save,
Be kind to me.

Spirits of the air,
Foul and dark, not fair,
Be kind to me.

Spirits of earthbound dead
That glide with noiseless tread,
Be kind to me.

Spirits of heat and fire,
Destructive in your ire,
Be kind to me.

Spirits of cold and ice,
Patrons of crime and vice,
Be kind to me.

Wolves, vampires, satyrs, ghosts!
Elect of all the devilish hosts!

I pray you send hither,
Send hither, send hither,
The great gray shape that makes folk shiver!
Shiver, shiver, shiver!
Come, come, come!

When the foul mixture in the cauldron begins to boil, the hooded figure lifts out a spoonful of murky liquid and sprinkles it around the inner circle. That done, he kisses the ground three times and puts out the fire.

No need to wait and see if the incantation has worked. He has never known it to fail.

CHAPTER 4

Lost in thought, Lila was eating—or, rather, not eating—when a girl named Karin Engals sauntered up to the girls' table and grinned at her.

"I saw Corey last night," she told Lila with a taunting smile. "He was looking kind of grim. Trouble in paradise?"

"Corey! I forgot all about Corey!" Lila gasped before she could stop herself.

Karin's smile became even broader. "Forgetting your boyfriend? That's not a good sign, chiquita. I guess the honeymoon is over."

Considering that you couldn't find a single person who really liked her, it was hard to explain how Karin Engals had become so popular. She never went anywhere without a pack of friends in tow. Maybe people were scared to say no to her.

Although she gave a general impression of prettiness, Karin had a thin, pointy face and sharp little eyes that always seemed to be looking for trouble. ("The weasel," Marci called her behind her back.) She was a great athlete, but she got furious when her teammates made mistakes. She was widely believed to plagiarize her term papers, but so cleverly that no teacher had ever discovered which books she'd stolen from. In grade school, she had been famous for pinching people. Pinching doesn't leave marks.

And it was no secret that she'd had her eye on Corey for a long time. "She's just waiting for you to let go of him for one second," Marci had once warned Lila. "Then she'll swoop down and grab him in her talons." To which Lila had answered, laughing, "Weasels don't *have* talons."

But there was certainly something predatory in Karin's expression as she stared down at Lila now. "How could you forget such a *cute guy*, Lila?" she cooed. "I mean, Corey's so *crazy* about you. Or is that all over?"

"Of course it's not over," Samantha said hotly

before Lila could answer. "Can't you see Lila's not feeling well?"

"Heartsick, I guess," was Karin's answer. "It's never pleasant when relationships start to go rocky."

I guess I've got to fend her off somehow, Lila thought. Life would turn truly unbearable if Karin started snooping around and pestering her. Aloud, she said serenely, "Corey and I don't live in each other's pockets, you know. We're secure enough that we don't have to spend every single second together."

"Yeah," Samantha blurted out. "You wouldn't understand, Karin."

"Well, Corey certainly wasn't looking very secure last night," Karin shot back. "He looked pretty upset to me. Maybe I was just imagining things, but . . ." She let her voice trail off and gave Lila a glance that was dripping with meaning.

"Where'd you see him?" Lila asked as casually as she could.

"Oh, I get around," said Karin.

"I bet you do," Marci muttered, just loudly enough for Karin to hear.

Karin reddened and glared at the three girls. "I *happened* to run into him in a *restaurant*, for your information. It was *not* that big a deal. But I can see I'm just wasting my time talking to you," she snapped.

"No kidding!" Marci said brightly.

Karin ignored her. She was glaring at Lila, and there was a hint of a threat in her face.

"Good luck with Corey," she said. "I have a feeling you'll need it." And she stalked away.

"What a lovely character," said Marci calmly. "You're so lucky she likes you, Lila."

"Are you going to put up with her?" Samantha said angrily. "You can't let her muscle in on Corey that way!"

Lila sighed. "I can't think about it now. I'll . . . I'll figure something out." She gave her soup a stir, then pushed her lunch tray away in disgust.

There was an awkward silence at the table.

"You know, Li," Marci finally said, "Samantha and I can't help you if you won't talk about what's the matter. You've been walking around like a ghost for two days now. Are you sick or what?"

Lila's eyes filled with tears. "Yes, I think *sick*

would be a good word." She ran a trembling finger over her lunch tray, fighting to keep her composure. "But I . . . I can't talk about it right now. I'm really sorry, guys. It's just too hard to explain."

"You don't have anything terrible, do you?" gasped Samantha.

Lila gave a watery laugh. "No. It's nothing like that. You're just going to have to trust me. I'll tell you when I can. If I ever can. Right now"—she stood up decisively—"I've got to track down Corey. There's something I need to tell him."

Note from Samantha Bardel to Marci Zwick:
> *I've got Picton for study hall. He's such a disgustoid. Speaking of disgustoids—I think Karin's out to get Corey, don't you? Lila better be careful. I hope Lila's okay though! She was acting so wierd at lunch. What do you think is going on? Maybe she's got her period! Or maybe . . . do you think she could be pregnant?*

Note from Marci Zwick to Samantha Bardel:
> *It's "weird," not "wierd." Anyway, I'm starting to get tired of worrying about Lila Lila Lila all the*

time. I mean, we all have problems— especially you. (Just kidding.) But why should she get all the attention when she gets a hangnail or something? Just because she's the most popular girl in school, everyone thinks everything has to revolve around her! I know I shouldn't say this, but I'm a little pissed off at Lila today. Even if she's in a bad mood, it wouldn't kill her to try to act like a normal person.

But you're right about Karin. She's working on something—I just know it. That little bitch—I mean weasel. Do they call female weasels "bitches," I wonder? It would suit her.

Lila finally found Corey putting some books into his locker. Even his back looked sad to her, and she felt another rush of guilt when she remembered the day before. "Hi," she said, touching his sleeve tentatively. "How are you?"

Corey took his time turning around. When he finally faced her, Lila saw that his eyes were squinched up with concern, like a child's. "How are *you?*" he asked. "That's more important. What happened last night? Are you mad at me?"

"That's the second time someone's asked me

that today," Lila said ruefully. "I'm not mad at *anyone*, Corey. Especially not you."

Corey reached out to touch her cheek—and Lila jerked back as though a moth had landed on her face. "Sorry," she said, trying to laugh. "You startled me." *So I still don't want him to touch me*, she thought dismally. *Well, I'm going to have to get over that. This is the guy I love.*

She gritted her teeth and put both arms around Corey's neck. "Give me another chance," she murmured. "I was feeling super-sick last night. I'm a lot better today."

"What was the matter, babe?"

"Oh, I don't know." She grinned coyly up at him. *What a fake I am*, she thought. "Hormones, or something. You know how girls get." *A sexist fake. Listen to me! How can he stand me?*

Corey certainly didn't seem to realize what she was thinking. "Actually, I don't know how girls get," he answered, his voice happier. "Maybe you can, you know, give me some lessons."

"Well, maybe," Lila forced herself to answer after a second. "What are you doing this afternoon?"

Corey looked surprised. "I've got practice, like always."

"Oops! That's right. Sorry. Well, do you want to do something tonight? After supper?"

"Great!" said Corey. "A walk in the woods?"

No! She couldn't face the woods again! "Mmm. It's a little chilly, don't you think?" Lila said. "How about if we just drive around?" She'd be able to keep Corey at a nice safe distance if he was driving.

"I'll pick you up at seven-thirty." Corey leaned down and gave Lila a gentle kiss. "Can't wait, babe. Now I've got to get to class. And so do you."

As he headed down the hall, his cheerful voice drifted back to her. "Should be a pretty night for a drive, with that full moon and everything."

"It's nice to see you again, Lila," Mr. Crawford said cordially that night at supper. He dabbed prissily at his lips with a starched white napkin.

"It's nice to see you, too, Dad," answered Lila. "How was your trip?"

"Fairly productive." Mr. Crawford never said anything was fine. He liked his speech to be extremely precise, which meant that when he traveled on business Lila always felt sorry for the people he'd be meeting. It couldn't be fun being lectured by a man whose every sentence sounded as though he'd written it out beforehand.

"Your mother tells me you've been feeling unwell," he continued. "What exactly seems to be the matter?"

Well, you see, I seem *to be acting like a werewolf, Dad.* Of course Lila didn't tell him that. "Just general cruddiness, I guess," she said, shrugging.

Mr. Crawford frowned slightly and dabbed his mouth with his napkin again. " 'General cruddiness' doesn't convey much to me. Can you be a little more specific, dear?" he asked.

I don't think that would be in my best interests, Dad. "It's not important, really," said Lila. "I'm just a little stressed out." Quickly she changed the subject. "Corey will be picking me up after supper," she told her parents. "We're going for a drive."

"Is all your homework done, dear?" asked her mother.

"Of course it is, Mom," Lila said impatiently. "I wouldn't go out if it weren't. You know that."

"Well, it never hurts to check," Mrs. Crawford

replied. And that ended the interesting part of the family's dinner conversation.

I live in a mausoleum, Lila said to herself as she rose to clear her plate. But right now, maybe that was better than having the kind of parents who realized you were alive, who actually paid attention to you. It meant you could hide things a lot more easily.

Silver-edged clouds were scudding across the black sky when Corey came to pick up Lila. The wind howled mournfully, as though it were looking for the moon the clouds had taken away. Dried leaves scuttled across the sidewalk as Lila and Corey hurried toward the car.

"It's nice and cozy in here," Lila said gratefully as she fastened her seatbelt. "Are we going anywhere special?"

"Nah, just cruising around," said Corey. "Unless you've got somewhere in particular you want to go," he added politely.

Lila couldn't help laughing. "You sound as though you're talking to my mother or something, Corey!"

"I just want to make sure you're happy," Corey said. "You know, we don't even have to go out if you're not feeling well. If your hormones are acting up, or whatever."

"I'm fine. Really. My hormones are fine. How'd practice go today?" Lila asked. Anything to get him off the topic of how she was feeling.

Corey brightened. "It went pretty good," he said. "I don't know what our chances are for this Saturday's game, but . . ."

Lila knew from experience that he'd keep going on this topic for a while. Usually she was happy to listen. After all, whatever made Corey happy made her happy, right? Tonight, though, she was relieved just to sink down in her seat, her mind a blank, and let his voice wash soothingly over her.

This was normal life. This was the way it should be. Lila and Corey spending a cozy evening together, homework all finished, talking about Saturday's game. (*One* of them talking about it, anyway.) Just two happy, ordinary high-school kids—content to be happy and ordinary—driving through a suburban neighborhood. Everything was bland and normal. There was nothing weird about either of them.

If last night happened at all, Lila told herself firmly, *it was just a quirk. It will never happen again. Look at me! I'm not insane, and I'm not some kind of monster, either! I'm just—*

"Whoa! There's the moon!" Corey's voice broke into her thoughts. "I guess it's clearing up outside after all. Is that what they call a harvest moon, Li?" He pointed through the left side of the windshield to where the moon, huge and golden, was hovering smack in the middle of the sky.

"How beautiful," Lila started to say. But she hadn't gotten past the first word before the moon's implacable stare hit her full in the face.

The instant its light touched her, Lila felt her scar beginning to throb and her skin beginning to crawl. The sensation was terribly familiar. After all, she'd experienced it only twenty-four hours before.

"It really happened," she whispered.

"What'd you say, babe?" Corey asked brightly.

Oh, no. I wasn't imagining last night. It's the moon that changes me!

Lila clenched her fists over palms that were already beginning to itch as they sprouted fur.

"Pull over," she said in a panic. *I can't let him see me this way!* "Pull over right here."

"Hey, what's the matter?" Corey asked, peering over at her. "You look kind of—"

"Corey! Just stop the car!" Lila shrieked. *It's going to happen any second!*

"Okay! Okay!" With a screech of brakes, Corey pulled over to the side of the road and stopped. Then he turned to Lila, his face half-worried and half-annoyed.

"What'd I do *now?*" he asked. "Geez, Lila! I thought we were having fun this time! Are you sick again? Is that it? Should I take you home?"

But Lila couldn't answer him. There was no time. Her body was about to explode, and her only conscious thought was that she couldn't be around Corey when it happened.

She wrenched open the passenger door and hurled herself out onto the road. For only a second she paused to get her bearings. Then she streaked away into the dark.

She was barely out of sight behind a tree when the transformation took place.

CHAPTER 5

It is much easier this second night. The instant the wolf exists, she is free. She knows where the woods are now and has no trouble finding them. And how friendly the moon is tonight, how golden and welcoming! Its mellow light shows her an endless tantalizing path through the trees, a path crisscrossed with hundreds of invisible tracks from the animals who have been there before. Invisible, but there all the same, for she can translate their various scents without any effort tonight. She is getting better at being a wolf.

At first she runs aimlessly, almost as if she were a human leafing idly through a book, stopping here and there to examine an illustration more closely. She tracks scents just to see where they'll take her. She scrambles to the top of a rocky slope to look down at the view. She splashes noisily through the brook for the sheer pleasure of getting her feet wet.

Somewhere deep she carries the unconscious knowledge of how to play, and playing is all she wants to do tonight.

Unfortunately, she won't get the chance. As the wolf is rolling puppy-like in a pile of deliciously scratchy pine needles, a new smell suddenly flickers across the edge of her senses. The wolf stops in mid-roll, then flips to her feet. She recognizes this smell. And yet . . . something is wrong.

It's a male human. She should get away, flee as fast as she can. But this is a human she knows. Smelling emotions is easy for the wolf, and she can tell that he is boiling with them. Fear? Anger? Confusion? She can't quite read them all. There are too many feelings flooding the air at once.

Somehow, though, she knows that the emotions are directed at her. How is that possible? What does she have to do with humans? Curious, she heads off to find the source of all these signals.

The scent is quite fresh. He must be nearby.

The wolf trots along intently, sniffing the trail. After a few minutes, she begins to hear the human as well. You can always recognize humans; they make so much noise. This one is crashing along like a bear. (Why? the wolf wonders. With all that moonlight, he should have no trouble seeing where he's going.) Suddenly he doubles back in his tracks and heads toward her, still so noisily that the wolf has no trouble slipping into the underbrush to watch him pass.

There he is. Young, she can see. Not fully grown yet, despite his height. Doesn't know she's here, and yet he's thinking about her. Can it be that he's looking for her? The wolf doesn't know why, but she suspects that he is.

Hunger begins to coil unbidden in her stomach.

Now, in her own mind, the thoughts start to battle. She has no need to fear this human. He doesn't want to hurt her. Indeed, the wolf has a confused sense that somehow she has hurt *him*, although she can't understand why this should be. Certainly he doesn't smell like an enemy.

He does, however, smell like prey. And the wolf can't help reacting to that.

Canids—members of the dog family—are programmed to eat whenever they get the chance. In the wild, they never know where their next meal will come from. It is to their advantage to bolt down large quantities of food whenever they find them. For this reason they are, basically, always hungry.

And this human is heading straight toward the wolf, with no idea that danger is waiting for him.

The wolf licks her lips hopefully. She doesn't think she can resist. The human would be simple to bring down, she is sure. One snap at his throat, and . . . She can almost taste him now.

No, she decides. She will not hold back.

She crouches down in the underbrush and prepares to spring. He is only a few paces away.

Like a silver streak the wolf leaps out and flies at the human, toppling him like a tree. His head hits the ground with a dreadful sound. The wolf's front paws pin down his shoulders before he has time to move. All she has to do is tear out his throat.

Just for an instant, though, she can't resist staring down at him. Let him realize what he's dealing with! Her glowing-green eyes bore into his terrified blue ones.

Terrified, yes. But the human is not as helpless as the wolf had thought. He stares back at her without flinching. He knows what's coming, and he's determined to accept it bravely.

It's the wolf who flinches instead. She hadn't expected this, hadn't known there was anything in a human's expression that could reach her. She is stunned in the presence of such despairing courage.

She is so ravenous she can hardly stand still, but some last vestige of human thought holds her back. With a sound that is almost a moan, she wrenches herself off the human and tears back into the underbrush.

The human lies motionless for a second. Then, painfully, he stands up, straightens himself, and staggers off down the path.

With hunger lashing at her insides, the wolf watches him stumble away. She wishes desperately that she could follow him. She wishes she understood why she's commanding herself to leave him alone.

As soon as he is out of sight, the wolf races off in the opposite direction. She is faint with hunger now. The first thing she needs to do is find some other creature to kill.

CHAPTER 6

"How are you doing, honey?"

Corey Ryan's mother paused in his bedroom doorway, tray in hand. On the tray were the three foods she always gave to her children when they were sick: Jell-O, crackers, and chocolate milk with a bendable straw. She had a feeling these comfort foods wouldn't do much for a seventeen-year-old who'd been attacked by a wild dog. But what were you supposed to offer your son in circumstances like this? A shot of straight whisky?

"I'm okay, Mom. The dog didn't even bite me," Corey said impatiently.

"They don't have to bite you to transmit rabies," put in his younger sister Hanny, sticking her head around the door behind her mother. "Did it drool on you or anything? Because drool can spread rabies, too. Like, if some saliva from a rabid animal mixes with *your* saliva, your chances of survival are—"

"That's enough from you, young lady," said Mrs. Ryan crossly. "It's almost ten-thirty. You should have been in bed ages ago. Asleep," she added, to forestall any chance of Hanny asking for a tray as well. "Now, scoot."

When Hanny was out of earshot, Mrs. Ryan walked into Corey's bedroom and put the tray down on his bedside table. "It *didn't* drool on you, did it?" she asked in a low voice. "Dad's calling Dr. Lamber to see if we need to take you to the emergency room. We should tell them if any saliva got on you."

Corey sighed ostentatiously. "The only thing that might need looking at, and I don't think it *does*, is my head, where I fell on it. I keep trying to tell you, Mom. That dog didn't hurt me. It only freaked me out. It didn't even *try* to hurt me."

"Didn't try to—Corey, you said it knocked you down and went for your throat!"

"I know, Mom, but it didn't bite my throat. It just kind of stared at me and ran away."

"Probably realized you were poisonous." Hanny, in her nightgown, had just poked her head into the room again. She took one look at her mother's expression and scurried away down the hall.

"I had the strangest feeling when I looked up at that dog," Corey said. He was staring up at the ceiling as though watching a rerun of what had happened to him. "I mean, it was a beautiful animal, a husky or something. Really pretty. Incredible green eyes. I've never seen a dog like it. And I was positive it recognized me. That's why it didn't hurt me. I just know it."

"No one I know has a dog like that," his mother said.

"Me either." Corey leaned back against his pillow. "That's what's even stranger. You see, I thought *I* recognized the dog, too. For a second there, we were almost, like, communicating."

He broke off and looked up at his mother rather sadly. "I guess that couldn't happen, huh?" he asked. "Must've been the bump on my head that made me think so."

"Probably, darling. Try and relax, now," his mother answered, and left the room quietly, careful not to let her son see the worry etched on her face.

"Well, hel-*lo*, Lila. How's Corey?" Karin Engals sauntered up to Lila as she neared her locker. The first bell was about to ring, and everyone was streaming into the building, slamming lockers, dropping books.

Lila shuddered inwardly as she remembered the way her drive with Corey had ended. "He's fine," she said carefully. No sense in letting Karin know anything, she thought. "We're doing just fine, thank you."

To her surprise, Karin was staring at her in genuine puzzlement. "No, I mean how's he *doing?*" Karin insisted. "How's he feeling? After the attack and all?"

Lila halted before her locker, staring at the other girl. "What attack?" she asked blankly.

"You haven't heard? I can't believe it!"

"Haven't heard *what?* Just tell me!"

"I can't believe it," Karin repeated meaningly. A sly smile played around one corner of her mouth. "*I* know. My *mother* knows. *Everyone* knows. I would have thought *you'd* be the first person he'd call. . . . Anyway, last night Corey was attacked in the woods by the reservoir."

"Attacked? By who?" Lila whispered. Her hands were beginning to shake. She hid them behind her back so Karin wouldn't see.

"Not by who—by what. A wild dog. It might've even been part wolf or something. It knocked him over and went for his throat, he said. He's lucky to be alive."

Lila was sagging against the wall, whitefaced. Her backpack clunked to the ground, but she didn't notice. *I can't breathe,* she thought. "Was he hurt badly?" she said faintly.

Karin looked almost disappointed at having to report good news. "Not really. The dog—or wolf or whatever it was—didn't bite him, anyway." The first bell rang then, but neither girl moved. "It just ran away. Corey's got a concussion, though. A mild one," Karin added reluctantly. "He didn't even want to go to the hospital, but his doctor thought he should. His head hit pretty hard when he fell. So he'll be in the hospital for a day or so, just for observation. No biggie. Still, it's *awfully* weird he didn't tell you about it right away. I wonder why he didn't? Guess it didn't occur to him." Karin looked at her watch ostentatiously. "Well, time for homeroom."

"Right," Lila told her, with an effort. "I'll . . . I'll get going."

But she didn't move. She just stood there, leaning against her locker and staring blankly into space. The school's front hall was emptying out now as the last few stragglers hurried toward their homerooms. A couple of kids glanced curiously at Lila as they passed, but she didn't even see them.

I attacked my own boyfriend last night. I could have killed him.

It had been hard enough to wake up that morning and realize once again that the same transformation had taken place in the night. Hard enough to come up with an explanation for why she'd sneaked in so late without bothering to inform her parents.

It had been hard enough trying to prepare another explanation—this one for Corey. How was she going to gloss over the fact that she'd bolted out of his car for no apparent reason?

A few minutes earlier, these problems had taken up all the mental space Lila had. But this new information blew them away like so many cobwebs.

Why don't I remember what happened?

Was the memory too horrible to face? Maybe it had been so traumatic that she'd blanked it out. Or did her perceptions change completely when she was a wolf? Lila had a dim vision of stalking *something*. Was it Corey? In her transformed state, did she stop recognizing people?

And would anyone make the connection between the "wild dog" and Lila herself?

They can't, Lila told herself firmly, and tried to brush the thought away. She hated herself for being so self-centered when she should be worrying about Corey. But she was frightened for her own safety all the same. *There's no way they could possibly know it was me. No one saw me transform. The only person nearby was Corey, and I know he didn't see anything.*

I hope he didn't, she thought with a sudden spasm of doubt. *I'm sure I got away out of sight before I . . .*

But what if Corey *had* seen her turning into a

wolf? What if he was keeping quiet about it for reasons of his own? Maybe that was why he hadn't called her.

This was worse than Lila could ever have imagined. *All right, so I didn't really hurt Corey this time,* she thought bleakly. But what would happen next time? How hideous an act would she commit? And would there be witnesses? Would anyone guess her terrible secret?

Tiredly, Lila rubbed her eyes and looked around. It was hard to believe that all around her normal life continued to go on. But it did.

"Goodness! You'd better get a move on, Lila. The second bell rang three minutes ago." Mrs. Doughty, the typing teacher, interrupted her brisk trot down the hall to frown at Lila.

"I . . . thank you, Mrs. Doughty." Lila's voice was weary. "I'm just going."

She couldn't stand here all day. But she couldn't spend much longer without some answers, either. That afternoon, when school was over, she was going to find out a few things about werewolves.

It's kind of like homework, Lila told herself with a

bleak attempt at humor. *Research. They're always telling us how important research skills are, aren't they?*

"Of a certainty several loathsome Aspects are common to every Werewolf. The Eyebrows are thick and long, meeting over the Nose with no Separation. His Teeth are of a reddish hue and sharp-pointed, like a Dog's; red, too, are his Fingernails, and of an Almond Shape. His Ears, lying far back on the Head, are uncommonly pointed. His Eyes and Mouth are dry; he suffers from dreadful Thirst and is likewise unable to weep. The Skin is scabrous and much scratched, and tending to hairiness . . ."

Lila shook her head. This was the ugliest account so far. Every book she'd found gave descriptions of werewolves, most of which were nothing like Lila herself, but none of them gave any real information about how they lived, how the transformations worked, information Lila could really use. Was there any point in looking through these books?

She had shaken Samantha and Marci loose after school. "You're going to the *library?*" they had asked incredulously.

Until today, Lila had never known about the library's occult section. Most of its titles seemed to be about poltergeists and the witches of Salem, but there were a few books about werewolves and vampires and other late-night movie characters. Half-scornfully, Lila had tried several before picking out *The Lore of the Werewolf.*

The book turned out to be a facsimile edition of an eighteenth-century work, complete with antique spelling and clumsy old woodcuts that looked more quaint than scary. So far, everything Lila had read was wrong, at least as far as it applied to her. She didn't match the physical description at all—except for things that didn't matter, like having fair skin and light-colored eyes. Plenty of people have those without being werewolves. Nor did she hate bright lights. Not that she'd noticed, anyway. She didn't have a constant craving for raw meat. (Not when she was a human, she thought uneasily.) She also wasn't extremely hairy, thank God.

These books have nothing to do with me.

What difference did it make if the lore was wrong, though? She had still turned into a wolf for two nights running, bright lights or no bright lights. . . . Lila flipped through the pages again to find out whether it said anything about what turned people into werewolves.

Here, again, the book couldn't tell her much, except that seventeenth-century Europe must have been a horrible place to live. According to the book, werewolves were possessed by the devil. So, too, were ordinary wolves, the author claimed: "Wolves are Demons, who verily prowl abroad in the Dark Hours, and urge Man to every kind of Lust and Murder, and to other infinite Crimes." He went on to explain how to torture suspected werewolves to death. And, for good measure, how to do the same thing to any real wolves unlucky enough to find themselves caught by humans.

People could also become wolves if they had been conceived during the time of a new moon. (*Gee, I'll have to ask Mom and Dad about that,* Lila thought sarcastically.) Sleeping on the ground could cause it, especially if there was a full moon on a Friday night. Drinking water from a wolf's footprint and eating a wolf's brains could also turn someone into a wolf, according to the book.

This whole book was so stupid and old-fashioned

it was starting to annoy her. She flipped through quickly to see if anything else was interesting.

The Wild Beast of Gevaudan was supposed to have killed hundreds of people, though the illustration made him look like a stuffed toy. . . . A peasant claimed his wolf hide grew underneath his skin, and he was sliced open to see if he was telling the truth. . . . Jacques Rollet, the werewolf of Caude, was trapped while still clutching bits of human flesh in his bloody hands.

Surely these were all nightmares, not true stories! Lila was about to return the book to the shelf when one series of especially gruesome woodcuts caught her eye.

The first showed a man strapped to a wheel, having something awful done to him with glowing hot pincers. In the second, he was being decapitated, and in the third, his headless body was being burned at the stake.

Gripped by fascinated distaste, Lila inexplicably found herself reading the text next to the woodcuts. The victim, she read, was a man named Peter Stubbe, a monstrously cruel murderer who was said to have flourished in the 1600s. He had apparently entered into a pact with the devil, and the devil had given him a magic belt that turned him nightly into a wolf, "strong and mighty, with Eyes great and large, which in the Night sparkled like unto Brands of Fire, a Mouth great and wide, with most sharp and cruel Teeth, a huge Body, and mighty Paws."

As a wolf, he had roamed the countryside inflicting so much carnage that people feared to leave their homes. And no wonder: "Oftentimes the Inhabitants found the Arms and Legs of dead Men, Women, and Children scattered up and down the fields, to their great grief and vexation of heart." *Probably an outrageous exaggeration*, Lila thought, but she kept reading. The child-victims, she saw with a sinking heart, had even included Stubbe's son. "He enticed the Boy into the Fields, and from thence into a Forest hard by, and there most cruelly slew him, and presently ate the Brains out of his Head. . . . Never was known a Wretch from Nature so far degenerate."

The tortures Stubbe had suffered when he was finally caught were even worse to read about than his crimes. After half a paragraph Lila was shaking with disgust. And maybe a little fear. She turned quickly to the next chapter so she wouldn't have to read any more about Peter Stubbe.

Maybe the character she was reading about had never really existed. Maybe he was just some poor, mad villain who'd inspired a folk tale that had grown to grotesque proportions over the centuries. Maybe he'd been innocent, frightened into making a fake confession. But Lila had no doubt that his punishment had been real enough.

What horrible things people did in the name of keeping the devil away! What dire fates had befallen people accused of being witches and werewolves and vampires over the centuries. Being burned and buried alive and walled up in dungeons—those things had really happened. But how true was the rest of it? Superstition might be something people laughed at nowadays, but none of its victims had laughed.

Of course that kind of thing doesn't happen nowadays, Lila reassured herself. *And anyway, it's not as though I'm some kind of crazed murderer.*

Even though you attacked your own boyfriend last night? a mocking voice inside her asked.

I didn't hurt him. Lila's justification sounded weak even to herself.

But what about next time? How can you know where this will end?

I'm not a murderer! Lila tried to overrule her rebellious thoughts. But her own relentless mind went on, *And I'm not the kind of person who tears up poor little animals, either.*

She pushed the hateful *Lore of the Werewolf* away and leaned her aching head against her arms.

Was she going to turn out like one of the sad, desperate creatures in the old stories? The nursemaid who'd slashed the throats of her charges, the werewolf princess whose subjects had thrown her down a well? Were the seeds of evil and madness sprouting ineluctably inside her at this moment?

How could she keep a secret like this hidden from other people? Would she learn to control it, or would she always be helpless in its grip?

When was it going to happen again?

From the records of Dr. Sean Lester, emergency-room physician

"Corey Ryan is a seventeen-year-old male who appears stated age. Patient was brought to the ER by his parents at 10:45 P.M., conscious but confused. Tells garbled story of attack by large dog, knocking him down and causing a concussion when he struck occiput. Maintains he never lost consciousness. Claims dog escaped after patient fell; denies dog bites. Close examination of skin reveals no sign of bites, lacerations, or other injuries. No indications of possible rabies contamination if, indeed, animal is rabid.

"Head shows contusion and swelling two centimeters behind right ear. Pupils unequal, left larger than right, variably reactive to light."

Dr. Lester laid down his ballpoint pen and rubbed his eyes. Twelve million cups of coffee since supper, and he was still dead on his feet. It had been a long night. A gunshot wound, a burst appendix, an amateur carpenter who'd hammered his thumb, two kids with ear infec-

tions, and a baby born in one of the ER chairs. And this kid's concussion. He checked the report for his name. Corey. He'd seemed like a nice kid, and not overimaginative. If he said he'd seen a wild dog, he probably had. The last thing this town needed was a rabid dog attacking people in the woods, but if the dog had raced off it was probably futile to alert the police. Still, he might as well give it a try. He wondered idly when he would see his first case of rabies in a human.

Dr. Lester finished his report on Corey Ryan and headed toward the nurses' station to use the phone. Unfortunately, he never got the chance to call the police. His second gunshot wound was about to arrive in an ambulance, where she'd managed to leave most of her blood. By the time Dr. Lester had seen to her, the wild dog had slipped his mind entirely.

CHAPTER 7

Lila was startled to see that it was almost five o'clock. She'd been buried in *The Lore of the Werewolf* for two hours. That meant she'd missed the late bus. She would have to walk home.

"I'm sorry, Ms. Clark," Lila apologized. "I didn't realize what time it was."

The school librarian smiled pleasantly from behind her desk. "You were concentrating so hard I hated to disturb you. But I suppose we'd both better clear out before the custodian comes in."

Lila was startled to see how normal everything looked outside. Two hours of reading about werewolves had skewed her worldview. This pleasant suburban street with its crisp autumn air was a bizarre contrast to the firelit world of torture and strewn limbs she'd just been visiting. It took several blocks of walking in the sunshine before she started to feel like herself again.

And it took several more minutes before Lila began to realize that she was being followed.

A motorcycle was purring along slowly a block behind her. Lila darted a quick glance over her shoulder. It was just enough to register that the driver looked young, that he was dressed in standard motorcycle-rebel black—and that he was darkly, strikingly, electrically handsome. Even from a block away, she could tell that she'd never seen anyone like him.

Have I seen him somewhere before? she asked herself. She couldn't believe she had. Yet, looking at him, she felt a thrill of recognition. *At last, at last,* some distant part of her mind was telling her. What did it mean?

Shaken, Lila turned around and quickened her pace. Behind her she heard the motorcycle picking up speed as well. It sounded as though it was only half a block behind her now. She glanced over her shoulder again. Yes, half a block, and the rider was staring at her in a way that made her knees weak. So he was following her. Well, she'd put a stop to that.

Strangely enough, she half-wished she could stop and wait for him instead. But of course she wouldn't give into an impulse like that. People got hurt that way.

Lila turned the corner and walked briskly down the new block. Only seconds later, the motorcycle caught up to her. It was hovering just behind her now, waiting, like some kind of predator. This time, Lila didn't have to turn around to know that the rider was staring at her. She had never felt so self-conscious in her life.

It's broad daylight, Lila reassured herself. *There are people outside everywhere. There's nothing this guy can do to me.*

But what did he want? This wasn't a motorcycle kind of neighborhood. In fact, Lila was disturbed to see that a couple of the adults working out in their yards were craning their necks anxiously. Clearly the motorcycle seemed as menacing to them as it did to her.

"Friend of yours?" a woman raking leaves asked Lila as she walked by.

Lila shook her head helplessly. "I've never seen him before," she said. *I don't think so, anyway.*

The woman pursed her lips and returned to her raking without a word.

"What does she think? I'm *luring* him down the block?" Lila muttered, walking even faster. She was coming up on a house she knew. The Parskys didn't mind kids cutting through their backyard to get to the next street. Whoever was on the motorcycle couldn't possibly follow her there through someone's yard. She'd get over to the next block and shake him off. All she had to do was duck along the side of the house and take the little path through their garden.

Unfortunately, Mrs. Parsky happened to be loading dishes into her dishwasher right at that moment. She looked out her kitchen window, saw Lila, and cranked open the window vigorously.

"Hi, Lila!" she called. "How's your mom?"

Uh-oh. "Hi, Mrs. Parsky," Lila answered as quietly as she could. "My mother is fine. She's—"

"I wish I could say the same for myself," Mrs. Parsky interrupted. "Ticker!"

"Excuse me?"

"My ticker," Mrs. Parsky explained, slapping her chest. "My heart. Giving me trouble."

Inside, Lila was dancing with impatience to be out of there. But she was cutting through Mrs. Parsky's yard, after all. She couldn't be rude.

"Oh, I'm so sorry to hear that, Mrs. Parsky," she said distractedly. She couldn't see the motorcyclist anywhere. He must have given up. With a little wave, Lila walked quickly toward Mrs. Parsky's back gate.

Once through the gate, Lila paused. Suddenly she wished, childishly, that she could go back and ask Mrs. Parsky if she could come in for a little while. Weren't there houses where schoolkids could stay if they felt threatened by bigger kids? Couldn't she do the same thing, just until she was sure the guy on the motorcycle had given up following her? But that would be silly. She had no reason to hide out anywhere.

You're being ridiculous, she told herself. *You see one guy on a motorcycle, and you imagine that he's tracking you down. You'd better not read any more werewolf books. They're making you paranoid.*

She headed down the driveway of the people who lived behind the Parskys and turned briskly toward home.

There was no sign of the motorcyclist at all. To her own disgust, Lila found herself feeling a little disappointed. He had given up awfully easily. Maybe he hadn't been following her at all. In fact, he *probably* hadn't been following her at all.

Look at you. You get totally agitated about some guy who doesn't have the slightest interest in you, who you don't even know, and you forget to think one thought about your boyfriend in the hospital. Pretty pathetic.

It was true that she hadn't remembered Corey once all afternoon. She'd have to call him the second she got home. But what was she going to say? They hadn't exactly parted on a friendly note. Lila was sure that was why Corey hadn't called her to let her know what had happened. He probably figured she was mad at him. It wouldn't have been like Corey just to drive away after she'd jumped out of his car in such a spectacular manner. He'd have been worried about her. He would have parked somewhere and gone off to find her. And look how she'd rewarded him.

Yes, she decided. She would call him right away and get it over with.

Lost in thought, Lila reached her own street

without realizing it. The half-hour walk seemed to have gone by in about thirty seconds. She was heading up the front walk when she heard the motorcycle again.

It was louder this time, as though its rider didn't care if she heard him. With a roar it pulled up right in front of her house. And stopped. And waited.

Slowly Lila turned around.

Staring straight into her eyes was the most mesmerizing person she had ever seen in her life.

He was about Lila's age, maybe a little older. Tall. Lean but muscular. Long black hair that fell across jade-green eyes. It was funny she could tell their color from so far away. Yes, he was dressed in standard-issue black leather, but on him it was as if he'd invented the look. A boy like this could never wear anything but jeans, boots, and a leather jacket.

Of course he hadn't bothered with a helmet. That kind of person never did.

Lila could hardly stand up. She felt as if the heat coming from his eyes was scorching her. He was staring at her as if he were waiting for something, but she couldn't move. It never occurred to her to speak to him.

He was still waiting.

Lila's heart was thudding in her throat so hard she couldn't breathe.

Gasping slightly, she forced herself to break the stare. Then, utterly helpless, she looked back at him again. The boy tilted his head speculatively, as if assessing her. Then he narrowed his gaze, sending a message she couldn't decipher. Slowly he turned his face away and throttled his engine, abruptly speeding away down the street.

Lila was furious to find that her legs were shaking so badly she had to sit down on the front step. What was the matter with her? She'd seen handsome guys before. She was acting like a fifth-grader with her first crush!

But she still couldn't help feeling as though she *did* know him already, as though on some level she'd always known him. As though she'd been waiting for him forever.

Would she ever see him again?

The late-afternoon sun dipped below the horizon. Shivering, Lila stood up and went into the dark house—where she stood indecisively in the front hall for a long time. She had no idea what to do with herself. All the adventure had evaporated from the day, leaving it flat and empty.

She completely forgot to call Corey.

Another country

It is almost dawn, but the brightening sky only points up the chill in the air more cruelly. On a hilltop stands a cauldron that was placed over a fire at midnight. The cauldron's unpleasant contents have had five hours to cool and freeze. Their power is gone now.

But already they have done their work. Thousands of miles away from that icy hill, a boy rides his motorcycle into a small town in America. He has been sent to find someone.

He has no idea where he will sleep tonight. He has no idea why he has been sent to that town, nor who sent him. He has never been there before. He has what he needs to get through the day, and no more.

Nineteen years old, and this boy has never known a home. He cannot even remember a time when someone was looking after him. It seems to him that he has always been on his own.

He no longer remembers a helpless, vulnerable baby boy who was stolen from his parents. Perhaps his memory has mercifully slammed shut on those horrifyingly tortured early years. Perhaps he only became aware of him-

self once he had been cast adrift in the wild by his guardian.

Perhaps there is a formless, forgotten part of him that longs disconsolately for the love and security he has never had, and will never have.

In any case, he has answered the summons. He has come.

CHAPTER 8

Lila paced back and forth in front of her bedroom window, waiting restlessly for the moon to rise. Three hours had passed since she had seen the boy on the motorcycle, and she was still too keyed up to do anything. She had fidgeted through her homework, pecked idly at her dinner, and taken a shower she didn't need, always trying to put the stranger out of her mind. It hadn't worked.

All she could think about was his face, the look of his hands, his eyes searing into hers. It was ridiculous to be so obsessed, she knew, and yet the few seconds of their encounter seemed infinitely more real than the drab, everyday world around her. She couldn't stop reliving them.

The scar on her leg was throbbing in its now-familiar way, and her skin was crawling. But just as on the previous evening, scudding clouds were covering the moon. Would the moon break through? Would she change into a wolf? And when? When?

It wasn't that she wanted to, exactly. But tonight the dark, restless world of the wolf matched her mood exactly. If she couldn't see the boy on the motorcycle again, even the bloodiest kind of danger was preferable to being trapped in her room. She needed something to snatch her out of herself. Lila had the feverish sense that change, *any* kind of change, was the thing she needed most desperately.

Just then there was a tapping on her bedroom door. Lila crossed the room and opened the door to find her mother.

As was often the case, Mrs. Crawford seemed to be simmering with barely repressed irritation. "There's a phone call for you, dear," she said. "Why on *earth* didn't you hear me calling?"

Lila's heart leaped despite herself. Maybe it was the boy who—no, he couldn't possibly know her number. He didn't even know her name—nor did she know his. "Who is it?" she asked her mother.

"Corey," her mother answered briefly. "Don't talk on the phone too long, okay?" Without another word she walked away down the hall.

Corey. Lila's heart sank with disappointment. There was no chance it could have been the other boy, but still . . . *I forgot to call Corey, too,* she thought guiltily.

Slowly she walked into the room across the hall and picked up the phone. "Hey, Corey!" she said brightly. "How *are* you? Are you at home?"

That sounded pretty convincing, she thought grimly. *You'd never guess I was the reason he was in the hospital in the first place.*

"Yup, I'm back home. The hospital just let me out. You heard about what happened, I guess?"

"I sure did! Uh, Karin Engals told me. I was so sorry to hear about it." *Now I sound too polite. Get some emotion into this!* Lila ordered herself. She thought briefly about asking Corey why he hadn't been the one to tell her, but she didn't really want to know the answer. "I kept meaning to call you," she went on, "but things got kind of crazy here this afternoon. You know how it is."

"Yeah." There was a pause—short, but long enough for plenty of things to go loudly unsaid.

It took everything Lila had to sound normal when she asked her next question. "Did they find the dog that, um, attacked you?"

Of course she knew they hadn't. She was just trying to find out if Corey suspected anything. But he couldn't suspect, could he? Lila could hardly believe the incredible truth herself.

"No, they didn't find it." Lila closed her eyes with relief. Corey hadn't questioned her use of the word "dog." That meant he wasn't thinking about wolves. She was still safe.

But his next words drenched her with a new fear. "It's kind of too bad they didn't find it right away," Corey went on. "Because the doctor said it's probably going to need to be destroyed. You can't let a vicious animal like that stay on the loose. But, I don't know," here his voice grew softer, "it's funny, even though it knocked me down and everything, it didn't really seem *vicious* to me."

I'm not *vicious!* Lila protested silently. "Destroyed," she repeated. "How?"

"Shot, I guess," Corey said slowly. "It's too bad. It was such a beautiful animal."

"Shot?" Lila felt a tidal wave of emotion washing over her. She was scared and angry, but most of all she felt an unreasoning terror that everything was closing in on her. As if she were a hunted animal at bay, enemies all around her. "Shot?" she repeated incredulously, defensively. "Don't you think that's a little extreme? It's a . . . a dog, Corey! Don't you care that an innocent animal might die?" Lila was on the verge of tears, so great was her distress.

Corey naturally picked up on it.

"Hey, wait a minute," Corey protested with a little laugh. "I'm the one you're supposed to be worried about, not some strange dog."

"Why should I be worried about you?" Lila countered swiftly. She wished she could stop herself, but she couldn't. All the confusion and frustration of the past days welled up inside her and spilled over in a torrent. She suddenly identified so strongly with those ancient wolves and helpless peasants, hunted by vengeful mobs. She was cornered and needed to lash out at her attackers, those who misunderstood her. With some vestige of wolf sense she could feel Corey's bewilderment in the silence on the other end. But still she went on, "You're okay, aren't you? The dog *didn't* bite you, did it? It ran away, right?" *I didn't hurt you, Corey, and I could have!* she wanted to shout. *I could have killed you! Instead I used every bit of self-control I had, and now you talk about destroying me!*

"Lila, are you mad at me?"

The question hung in the air.

"Because you sure sound it," Corey added. "And *I* sure don't have any idea why. I was looking for you in the woods last night, you know. That's why I got attacked."

"Oh, so it's *my* fault you got attacked!" Lila didn't even think about how strange the words sounded. She was too caught up in panic to hear herself, too swept with fury at Corey's lack of perception. He hadn't done anything to hurt her. He really hadn't. But he understood so little about her agony that Lila suddenly wanted to throttle him.

We're worlds apart, she reminded herself. *Maybe we always were, and I just never saw it until now. But*

Corey's so . . . uncomplicated, it's as if he's a different species. Poor guy.

She felt ancient compared to him.

"It's not your fault. I'm not saying it's your fault." Corey's voice was very gentle. "But Li, why'd you cannonball out of my car like that, anyway? You really scared me."

Here it was, and she didn't have an answer ready.

"I know something's going on with you. Can't you tell me what it is?" he asked softly, sadly.

Not even a fraction of it.

What she did want to say shouldn't be said over the phone. It was time to tell the truth.

Not the whole truth, of course. She couldn't tell him that. But it wasn't fair to keep him hanging around when whatever feelings she'd once had for him had evaporated entirely.

In a way, she still loved him. But it was a wistful love, the kind a child might feel for a cherished plaything now outgrown and lying lonely on a shelf. Because Lila had outgrown Corey. Something had pushed its way into her life and changed her so utterly and irrevocably it was almost impossi-

ble to imagine how normal everything had been
. . . before.

Corey was the perfect boy for the girl Lila used to
be—and would never be again. Part of her felt sad
to leave him behind. But in a deeper, hidden part
of her, she couldn't really feel sorry. As much as her
secret horrified her, Lila's spirits leaped and soared
with every transformation. It made her feel alive as
never before. And nothing in her old life could ever
come close.

"Listen, Corey, I can't really go into it now," Lila
faltered. "My mom needs the phone. Maybe we
could talk tomorrow? In person?"

Lila would wait until then. It certainly wasn't fair
to break up with someone over the phone.

"Well, okay," Corey said after a second. For the
third time, a pause came up like a wall between
them. "Not tomorrow, though. I won't be in
school. The doctor thinks I should stay home one
more day."

"Day after tomorrow, then. I'll meet you on the
front steps after school." *We'll end everything then.*

"Lila?"

"Yes?"

"I love you."

"Me, too," Lila managed to get out. She hung up the phone before he could hear her choking sobs.

She is surrounded by fog—swimming in it, choking in it. Where is she standing? There are no sights, no scents to offer any clues. Everything looks different; everything smells different.

Someone is calling her name, and she is here to find him.

She has a confused sense that the one she's looking for is nearby. But there are so many barriers between the two of them! These thin, fingerlike branches winding their spidery tendrils around everything—what are they doing here? She can barely make them out through the fog, but they're everywhere. She takes a tentative step forward, and one clammy stalk twines around her ankle while another coils around her neck. She shudders and pulls backward, but there are just as many groping branches behind her. Retreating won't help anything.

And the hideous, sucking ground beneath her feet! Every time she takes a step, she feels herself starting to sink. If she stands still too long, she can feel the muck rising up around her ankles with frightening speed. This place wants to keep her here, she can tell. It won't let her out without a fight.

A small animal of some kind scuttles across her foot and disappears into the fog. She hears it scream thinly as something lurches forward and grabs it. Then she is alone again.

Lila . . .

Is it her real name she hears? Or is it the wordless call of another being's emotion? She isn't sure.

I need you.

Again, she isn't sure whether she heard the words or just felt them. Whichever, she can absolutely feel the pain behind them. The pain and the power. This is a being far stronger than she. Even his loneliness is stronger than hers. He is calling her out of a pit of despair so deep that no one can rescue him. And his need for her is irresistible.

I would die for you, she finds herself thinking, and begins to walk toward the voice.

The protesting branches coil around her. The

ground churns under her feet. She doesn't care. Dying in this forest would be worth it, as long as she were fighting her way toward him.

She can feel him getting closer. Is he trying to reach her, too? Her heart begins to thud with painful excitement.

I'm coming, she tells him joyfully.

Now she is sure she can hear his breathing—fast and shaky, as though he's as excited as she. The very air seems to heat up around her. To her amazement, she sees that the twisted branches in her path are starting to lift out of the way like curtains on a stage. The ground, too, is firmer, and the mist is beginning to clear. She can make her way forward with confidence.

He is very close. She knows it. *Yes, yes, I'm here,* she calls to him dizzily. In a second she will see him. Half-joyous, half-terrified, she reaches out through the branches to touch him.

With a rending screech, the ground in front of her opens up and she plunges forward into a black chasm.

"No!" Lila gasped, and woke up.

She was lying on her bed, fully dressed, damp with sweat, and trembling uncontrollably.

"No," she said brokenly, feeling as if the pain would actually rip her heart in two. "It couldn't have been a dream. I won't *let* it be a dream!"

She closed her eyes, hoping desperately to recapture the experience of a few seconds before. But when she lifted her head and looked around again, she saw only the hateful blandness of her bedroom.

So it *had* been a dream. In real life, there was no one out there looking for her. In real life, she lived in this neat, loveless room. She was her nothing self again, with nothing to look forward to. She hadn't even become a wolf this time.

To think that I'd be disappointed by that, Lila thought dryly as she got up from the bed and dragged herself over to her window. Glancing out, she saw that the moon was beginning to wane. Its lopsided face stared cruelly down at her. *Nothing left for you,* it seemed to say.

The full moon was over. That must be why she'd stayed herself tonight. Strange how flat and lifeless she felt in her own skin.

On the fourth night, nothing happened to Lila at all, though she lay awake all night waiting.

I'll have to see what happens next month, she thought, with a secret thrill of joy.

Immediately she was disgusted with herself. How could she be looking forward to such a revolting change? Was the transformation in her body beginning to take hold of her mind, too?

You should be ashamed, Lila said to herself. But the admonishment couldn't touch the part of her that now mattered most.

The dream had changed everything.

CHAPTER 9

"You are absolutely, totally out of your mind," Marci announced.

It was the morning after the fourth night. School would be starting in a few minutes. Lila stood before her locker, Samantha and Marci in front of her. It was almost as if they were trying to block her in, keep her from doing anything they didn't agree to first.

Lila had just told them she was going to break up with Corey after school. Neither of her friends was taking the news well.

"I can't believe this. I can't believe how stupid you're being," said Marci in rapid-fire bursts. "Corey's perfect for you! You guys are the absolutely perfect couple!"

"Not if—not if I don't think so," Lila replied. "It

takes two people to make a perfect couple, you know."

"But he's so cute!" wailed Samantha. "How can you just *abandon* someone that cute?"

Lila gave an exasperated sigh. "I'm not abandoning him. He'll survive. It's just—I don't know. There's something missing between us. No matter how cute Corey is."

Marci squinted at her suspiciously. "You're blushing," she said quietly.

"No, I'm not!"

"Yes, you are," said Samantha with interest. "You look like a beet." She shook her finger teasingly. "Someone's got a secret! Someone's got a secret!" she chanted. "Someone's got a—"

"Oh, all *right,*" Lila snapped. "If you really want to know, I did happen to see this other guy. But there's nothing going on between us. I don't even know him." Quickly she described her encounter with the boy on the motorcycle. "We didn't even talk or anything," she finished. "It's just . . . seeing him made me realize there's—I don't know—some potential out there that I'm missing."

"Yeah, really." Marci's voice was withering.

"Someone you don't even know and probably won't ever see again certainly offers you a lot of *potential*."

Lila was silent.

"You're losing it," said Marci.

"You're not being very nice about this." Lila bit off the words. "We're *friends*, aren't we? Why can't you be more understanding?"

Marci pinched her lips together and exhaled hard, as though she were trying to control herself. "Of course we're friends," she continued in a calmer voice. "And that's why I'm upset, Li. I'm not trying to shoot you down. I just don't like to see you making a fool of yourself over something that's totally imaginary."

"Besides, Corey really loves you and everything," Samantha put in. Her blue eyes were wide and anxious. "Remember 'The Wizard of Oz'?"

"What about it?" asked Lila blankly.

"You know how, at the end, Dorothy's talking about how there's no place like home, and if you're looking for happiness you'll find it in your own backyard or whatever? So all I'm saying is, Corey's in *your* backyard. Wouldn't you be, you know, happier if you just stayed with him?"

"Maybe I would. Maybe I would! But right now, I don't feel that way. I mean, God, I'm only sixteen years old! Do I have to settle down with Mr. Sensible for the rest of my life *right this minute?*"

"Corey is perfect for you," Marci said again, shaking her head pityingly. "You might as well face it."

"*You* think he's perfect for me. Samantha thinks he's perfect for me. My parents probably think he's perfect for me, too, if I cared what they thought. But guys, *I* don't think so! Doesn't that count for anything?"

"Not when you're being crazy," said Marci stubbornly. "Not when you're throwing everything away."

"Excuse me?" Lila said. "Am I missing something here? I don't want to be in this relationship anymore. Period. You're my friends. I expect a little support, at least!"

Marci didn't answer that. Instead she switched to a different tack. "You don't even trust your own best friends anymore," she said. "You think we're out to sabotage you. You think we don't care about what's best for you."

"I think you care," Lila said carefully. "I'm just not sure you *know*. I'm really the only person who can know what's best for me."

"You know what, Lila?" answered Marci. "I pity you. I really do. You think you're doing what's best for you, but you're really being selfish to a really nice guy who cares a lot about you. It's going to be hard explaining this to people."

And she swept away, obviously proud of having gotten in the last word.

After a doubtful glance at Lila, Samantha followed Marci.

The first bell rang. Lila absently gathered her books together and started down the hall.

She had never realized before that her friends felt threatened by the thought of her doing something that didn't fit the plan.

This day is starting out just great, she thought bitterly. *Let's hope things improve from here.*

They didn't. There was still Corey to talk to.

All day long Lila dreaded the time when she'd have to confront him. Once, when she passed him in the hall, his eyes met hers briefly and then flicked away. Lila was sure he sensed what was coming.

When she walked slowly out onto the front steps after school, Corey didn't see her at first. He was staring out at the school lawn, which was scattered with couples leaving school together.

For a second Lila just stood there watching him. Was he remembering the time when he and Lila had first started going out? She felt as though she could recall every second of those early days. Back then, she'd thought of Corey the instant she woke up every morning. She had constantly found herself smiling. Every night she had replayed their conversations over and over in her mind as she lay in bed. She hadn't needed any sleep; she had just floated through her days. Corey had been everything to her.

When was that? I feel a hundred years older now.

Maybe Samantha and Marci were right. Maybe she was making a mistake. Corey was so nice and so good at things. The two of them were perfect for each other, everybody said so. . . .

If a motorcycle hadn't passed in front of the

school just then, Lila might have changed her mind. The rider wasn't the boy she'd seen the day before; he was a middle-aged delivery man in a yellow jumpsuit. Even so, the way her heart jumped at the sound made her certain she was doing the right thing. If a total stranger on a motorcycle turned her upside down, then she shouldn't be spending any more time with Corey. It would only remind her of what she was missing.

I don't care if I never see that other boy again. I'd rather remember the one time he looked at me than spend the rest of my life with Corey.

The thought was shocking to her. She hadn't wanted to admit the strength of the mystery boy's hold on her. Now that she knew, it was time to get this over with.

She walked forward and put her hand on Corey's shoulder.

He turned without surprise and smiled quizzically at her. "I miss you already," he said wistfully.

Lila couldn't smile back. Biting her lip, she took his hand. They walked down the school steps silently, side by side. At the bottom, Corey cleared his throat. "Where to?" he asked.

"We can just walk around the block, I guess," Lila said helplessly.

They walked a way together in silence before Corey spoke again.

"I know what you're going to tell me, Lila. I just want to know why you're doing it."

"I wish I could tell you." Lila's voice was bleak. "I'm not right for you any more, Corey."

"*I* think you are," he said, "and I should know, shouldn't I?"

Lila remembered that she'd said almost the same thing to Samantha and Marci. "You're right about what you're feeling," she said, "but you don't realize how much *I've* changed. It's not that I wanted to. Believe me, it would be a lot better if things could have stayed the way they were."

"Why *can't* they stay the same?" asked Corey sadly. "I'm willing to forget what's happened—whatever *has* happened. I mean, every couple has problems they have to work out. If we love each other, we can work *anything* out, can't we?"

Lila didn't answer.

"Can't we?"

"No, we can't," Lila said. "I-I do love you. But

not in a way that will do anything for either of us."

Corey stopped on the sidewalk and stared at her. "What's *that* supposed to mean?" he blurted.

"It means I don't love you in the right way anymore." Feeling suddenly restless, Lila started walking again, but Corey reached out, grabbed her wrist, and turned her to face him.

"When people tell you something like that," he said slowly, "it usually means they've started loving someone *else* in the right way. Is that what you're saying?"

"No." Lila tried to pull away, but Corey wouldn't let go. "I swear there's no one else. I mean, who could there be?" Her voice was getting shrill. She did her best to lower it. "Corey, you see me every day," she continued more calmly. "You *know* you're the only person I'm involved with."

It wasn't really a lie, after all. No one could call her "involved" with the guy on the motorcycle. She'd probably never see him again anyway.

"And I also know what a great person you are," Corey continued. He was starting to sound more confident. "So if you're not involved with someone else, then there really isn't a problem. God, what a relief! You know, I was sure you were going to tell me you'd fallen for some college stud or something. But if you haven't, then there's no reason you can't give *us* another try."

Before Lila could think up an answer, Corey was pulling her even closer. "I'm sure I can change your mind, babe," he murmured huskily. His lips nuzzled her hair, then moved toward her mouth. "After everything we've been through—"

Get away from me, Lila's pulse beat frantically. *Get away from me. This is sacrilege. Get away from me.*

"Don't you dare touch me!" she cried out in panic. She jerked violently out of his arms. "I mean it," she panted. "Keep away, Corey."

"My God." Corey was pale. "You *do* mean it."

"Yes. *Yes.* What does it take to make you believe me?"

Corey shook his head in disbelief. "You don't even want me to touch you," he said in a stunned voice.

Lila was still breathing hard. "That's right. I don't. I'm sorry, but I don't. You're a really nice guy, but—"

"But I turn your stomach. Why didn't you explain it *that* way?" Corey asked bitterly.

"Hey, it's not that bad." Lila tried to smile. "I just don't—"

"Shut up, Lila," Corey broke in harshly. "I can see what you don't want. Okay? You've made your point, okay? God *damn* it, don't keep rubbing my face in it!"

Suddenly he rubbed his eyes with the back of his hand and turned away. "You're pretty amazing, you know that?" he said brokenly. "All this time you really had me believing you loved me."

"Corey, I—"

He wouldn't let her finish. "I don't know what you wanted from me, Lila. But you can just forget it. I'm not hanging around so you can make a fool of me. You can just go to hell." His voice was ragged. "Don't you ever come near me again."

Half-stumbling, he began to walk away.

Lila stood motionless, watching him go. When he turned the corner, she slowly headed toward home.

It was over. She should have been relieved, but she didn't feel anything at all.

She kept hearing Corey's last words to her.

You can't send me to hell, Corey. Believe it or not, I'm there already.

When Lila was halfway home, the boy on the motorcycle drove by. He didn't stop this time. He gave her a piercing look over his shoulder and sped away without once looking back.

How it happened

History is full of stories about human children being raised by wild animals. Few are true, although everyone wishes they were. Who can bear the thought of a child being abandoned in the wild? Much easier to comfort oneself imagining a world so loving that its fiercest creatures will happily adopt any baby they find.

In the boy's case, the wild was infinitely kinder than the being who had raised him, the only parent he'd ever known. Nothing nature did to him could ever be as cruel or unpredictable. When he escaped, he spent his first few days of freedom fearing only that the guardian would come back for him. Once the boy understood that the other was never coming back, he felt safe for the first time.

Out in the wild he lost the stooped, frightened look he'd had as a child. Extremes of cold and heat stopped mattering to him. He learned to eat whatever he could find whenever he could find it. He learned, too, the habits of the other creatures sharing the woods and fields with him.

The boy never bothered the animals. It wouldn't have occurred to him to try to befriend them; he was so lonely he didn't even know he was lonely. But he did like to watch the animals when they let him.

He liked the wolves, especially. To the boy, who had no idea what a family was, the wolves' interaction with one another was astonishing. And after the "rescue" was over and he'd been set free for the second time, it was to the wolves that he returned. He liked to think that some of the older members of the pack remembered him.

So when his transformation took place, it seemed completely normal to him.

Now he feels as though he only comes to life during the full moon. The rest of the time, he is a shadow. Which is why, of course, it is easy for him not to care that his life is as empty as it is.

It doesn't feel as empty now, though. This girl has recognized him. He is sure of it.

It's only a matter of time.

CHAPTER 10

When you're suddenly without a boyfriend and your best friends are ignoring you, you have plenty of time to think about things. On her own most of the time, Lila began to wonder why she'd been chosen—if that was what it was—to become a werewolf. Why had this happened to *her*?

Could it be heredity? Lila was absolutely positive that neither of her parents had a trace of werewolf blood. Naturally she had no proof of this, but the idea was inconceivable all the same. Still, there might be ancestors who'd carried the gene. Perhaps, by some cruel chance, werewolfism had been passed down through the generations and come alive again in Lila.

Or was becoming a werewolf somehow contagious? If so, why had Lila caught it, and from whom? Surely she was the only person she knew with this problem.

Werewolves could spread their condition to humans, of course. Though the books Lila had read all claimed there were different ways for this to happen, there seemed to be general agreement that being attacked by a wolf or werewolf could transform an ordinary human being into a werewolf as well. But Lila had never been attacked by a wolf.

Or had she? She certainly didn't remember any kind of attack. For the first time, though, Lila wondered exactly how she'd gotten the scar on her leg. The scar had begun to fester before anything else about her had transformed. Perhaps it held the clue to her condition.

"Mom," Lila asked that night at supper, "how did I get this scar on my leg?"

Mrs. Crawford dropped her fork with a clatter. She darted a quick glance at her husband and looked down at her plate, her face working strangely.

"It's not a *disfiguring* scar, dear," her mother

finally said. For some reason she sounded defensive. "It's hardly visible at all. You can always wear pants if you're worried about it."

"I'm not worried about it," Lila said in surprise. *Not most of the time, anyway.* "I was just wondering about it, that's all. I mean, you may not even know how I got it."

"I do know." Mrs. Crawford's voice was pinched with discomfort.

At the other end of the table, Mr. Crawford had broken off eating and was staring into midair with a glassy gaze, almost as if he was reliving some painful memory from the past. *What is going on with these two?* Lila wondered.

"It was when . . ." Mrs. Crawford broke off. "You remember that we lived in France for six months when you were little?"

"Just bits of it," Lila answered. Her father had been there on business, she knew. "I remember the food. Someone used to give me rolls with chocolate inside."

"That would have been Genevieve," her mother said. "A local girl. She took care of you two afternoons a week."

"And I remember a place all covered with flat stones. A playground?"

"A courtyard," answered Mrs. Crawford. "It was in front of the house we were renting. You used to play out there. In fact, it was there that . . . it happened."

"What happened?"

Mrs. Crawford wiped her mouth with her napkin and pushed her plate away. "You had a little doll," she said slowly. "Do you remember her?"

"I don't think so."

"You just adored that doll. You called her Croaky, for some reason. You took her with you everywhere, and you wouldn't go to sleep without her.

"But one day, one very cold winter day . . ." Mrs. Crawford took a deep breath. "You forgot your doll. You left her outside in the courtyard. You didn't remember her until bedtime. And then you had a fit.

"Well, I felt I couldn't give in about something like that," Lila's mother went on. "If I had found the doll for you, it would have sent a very negative message."

"What kind of negative message?" asked Lila wonderingly.

"That you could just go around forgetting things and expect others to take care of them for you. That you didn't need to be responsible for your own possessions. That all I was there for was to clean up after you. That's what all the books told us."

"Mom, I was three years old!" Lila protested. "Three-year-olds expect other people to take care of them because other people are *supposed* to take care of them!"

"Don't, Lila. I've had plenty of time to be sorry since then without help from you," said her mother wearily. "Anyway, I sent you to bed. I told you there would be plenty of time to find the doll in the morning.

"But you didn't want to wait that long," Lila's mother continued. "So you waited until your father and I had gone to bed. And you sneaked out of the house.

"I don't know what woke me. I must have heard the front door squeak. I got up and found that you weren't in your room. I walked to the front door and . . ."

Mrs. Crawford's voice faltered.

"You were outside in your nightgown and bare feet. It was well below freezing. You had gone out to look for your doll. And when I found you, you were at the bottom of the steps with the doll in your hand. And a . . . a wolf was attacking you."

"A wolf," Lila echoed in a whisper.

"I don't know where it came from," Mrs. Crawford went on rapidly. "We lived in a perfectly civilized little town. We weren't out in the forest somewhere. A wolf in a place like that was a total anomaly."

Lila's father spoke up for the first time. "The police said it was unprecedented for a wolf to attack within the town's limits," he said sternly. He sounded to Lila as though he was profoundly displeased with the wolf for ignoring tradition. "They'd never seen a case like that before."

"I ran down the steps and grabbed you away, naturally," Lila's mother recounted.

Lila stared at her mother, openmouthed. She'd

never told this story before, but now as Lila heard it, all sorts of bells were going off inside her.

"Mom, weren't you scared?" she burst out. She couldn't imagine her mother confronting a wolf in the dead of night.

"I was scared for you, Lila," her mother said firmly. "It never occurred to me to worry about the wolf, huge as it was. I realize now that I must have exaggerated its size in the terror of the moment, but it seemed enormous. Compared to the wolf, you were the size of a tiny doll," she said musingly. "All I could think was to save my baby."

"And you did," Lila finished in a whisper. What had happened, she wondered, to that hopeful, heroic young mother? It was almost impossible to see her in the rigidly controlled, undemonstrative woman Mrs. Crawford was now.

"I don't know how I did it exactly, because it seemed the wolf was actually upon you," Mrs. Crawford went on dreamily. "But I felt stronger and faster than I'd ever felt before in my life. I ran down, snatched you up, and had us both safely inside before I knew it."

"You saved my life?" All these years, Lila had

never known. Not just about the attack, but about what her mother was capable of. *I guess she does care about me,* Lila thought as the truth suddenly dawned clear as day. *She just can't show it,* she finished sadly. *Now, after all this, I find out.*

Now her mother shook off her mood of reminiscence and became the brisk, no-nonsense person Lila had known every day of her life.

"The wolf didn't seem to have bitten you," Lila's mother went on. "It only scratched your leg. But the scratch was bleeding rather severely, so we took you to the hospital in the next town.

"They worried that the wolf might be rabid," she said. "I pointed out that it hadn't bitten you, but they were inclined to be very cautious in a case like this. So you had to have a series of rabies injections. Don't tell me you don't remember *those!*"

Lila shook her head.

"Well, you certainly carried on enough about them at the time," said Mrs. Crawford. "I thought we'd go deaf listening to you. And of course it was all for nothing, just as I'd told them."

It's okay, Mom. You don't have to act concerned for my benefit.

"It was a very distressing time for all of us," said Lila's father. "Really, I found it impossible to think about France in the same way after that. I was frankly glad to come home."

"I was, too," agreed his wife. "Once we were back home, I was able to put it all out of my mind." She turned to Lila. "Well, that's the story of your scar," she said briskly. "Do you have any questions?"

"Besides why you and Dad aren't sorry that this happened to me, you mean?" Lila asked angrily. "Gee, I'm sorry that I inconvenienced you both so much. Ruining France for you and everything."

"Don't you take that tone with me, young lady!" Mrs. Crawford snapped. "Naturally we were terribly sorry that this happened to you. I'm only sorry I allowed you to become so dependent on that ridiculous toy. If I'd been more conscientious, the whole thing could have been avoided."

Conscientious about a three-year-old's favorite doll? It seemed like a strange priority to Lila. But surely there was no point in upsetting her mother further, not now that Lila had the information she'd wanted.

"Just one other thing," she said quietly. "What happened to the wolf?"

Her father answered this time. "Oh, it disappeared," he said. "They never found it. But in the next town, only a few kilometers away, it killed someone the following night. So you can see how lucky you were, actually."

"I certainly can," Lila murmured. Neither of her parents noticed her tone.

By mid-month, Lila's mysterious stranger had started coming by every day. Sometimes the sound of the motorcycle purring would wake Lila in the morning, just seconds before her alarm clock. By the time she got to her bedroom window, motorcycle and rider would always be gone.

Once he passed by her school as she was dozing drowsily through American history. Lila sat bolt upright, startled, and then dashed to the window without thinking. She could just make him out turning left at the intersection in front of the school before the motorcycle vanished from view.

"I assume you're looking for the Dred Scott decision out there, Lila," said Mr. Heyer, the teacher, irritably. "That being the topic of our discussion, as you are no doubt aware."

"I'm really sorry," said Lila. She could feel herself reddening. "I was—I thought I heard—well, anyway, it won't happen again."

Karin Engals snickered. As she returned shamefacedly to her desk, Lila was glad to see that Marci, who was also in the class, didn't even crack a smile. At least Marci hadn't turned her back on her completely.

After class, though, Marci made her way toward Lila as they headed for the door.

"It was the same guy, wasn't it?" she asked knowingly.

"What same guy?" Lila said, pretending innocence.

"Come on, Li. You know what I'm talking about. I heard the motorcycle. It was that guy you told us about, right?"

"Of course not." Lila tried to laugh it off. "I just lost my mind for a second—kind of dozed off. You know how it is when you're crazed with boredom."

Marci peered at her suspiciously. "You don't

want me to know about that guy, do you? You're
trying to keep him secret."

"Marci, there's nothing to know. I only saw him
once. I've never even spoken to him!" Lila hoped
she didn't sound as flustered as she felt. For some
reason, she didn't want Marci to know that the boy
on the motorcycle was coming around so often.
Partly it was because she felt as though mentioning
such phantom visits—pinning them down with
words—might somehow jinx them. *Besides, he
doesn't want me to tell,* she thought, unsure how she
knew. *We're in this together.*

Whatever "this" was.

Very late that night, the sound of the motorcycle
broke into Lila's sleep. Without realizing what had
awoken her, she sat up groggily.

"What's that?" she murmured.

Then the engine cut off abruptly, and Lila realized what the noise had been.

A throbbing silence descended on the house. On
bare feet Lila walked softly to the window and
peered outside. It was a dark, windy night. She
couldn't see the motorcycle anywhere.

But the boy was standing under her bedroom window, his face turned up to hers. Some trick of the light made his eyes glow a luminous green, like a cat's, as she stared down at him.

"Lila," he said once, and disappeared.

A second later, she heard the motorcycle drive away.

The street was quiet again. No lights in any of the houses. Lila shivered. What was she doing here at the window? Had she imagined his visit?

How could he have known her name?

I must have had another dream, she thought wistfully, and returned to bed.

Lila might never have remembered the event if her mother hadn't mentioned it the next morning.

"I thought this was supposed to be a *quiet* neighborhood," Mrs. Crawford said irritably as she poured herself a cup of coffee. "If we're going to start having motorcyclists riding up and down the street at two in the morning, we may as well move."

"It didn't bother me," said Lila's father. He could sleep through anything. "How about you, Lila?

"Lila?" he repeated. "What's the matter?"

Lila was staring at her parents in shock. So it hadn't been a dream after all.

"He was really here," she murmured to herself.

"Who was? What do you mean?" asked her mother quickly.

Don't tell her. "Nothing," Lila answered. "All I meant was, I heard the motorcycle, too, but I thought . . . it was a dream."

"Well, I hope that's its first and last visit," said Mrs. Crawford firmly.

Lila didn't answer. She couldn't.

He was coming for her.

CHAPTER 11

"I never seem to see Corey around these days," remarked Lila's mother one Saturday night. She was cutting up vegetables for a stew, and Lila was helping her in the kitchen. "Where's he keeping himself?"

Lila opened the refrigerator to take out a package of stew beef. "He's been awfully busy," she said without turning around. "The coach is really working them hard, I guess."

She couldn't bear discussing Corey with anyone. Not with her friends, and certainly not with her mother. It wasn't that she missed Corey, exactly, although after spending three Saturday nights in a row at home with her parents Lila was beginning to wonder whether she might have been a little hasty to leave him without making other plans for herself. It was more that Corey still looked so *flinching* whenever he saw her that Lila felt as guilty as she did.

But she didn't want to share these thoughts with her mother, who had fortunately gone on talking.

". . . always thought he was a nice boy," Mrs. Crawford was saying. "Certainly presentable, and very polite to your father and me. What are his parents like? Do you know, in all this time I've never met them?"

"Corey's parents, you mean?" asked Lila blankly as she picked up a butcher knife to begin cutting up the stew meat.

"Yes, of course Corey's parents," said Mrs. Crawford. "Who else have we been talking about? I was just thinking that when Corey stops being so busy, maybe your father and I ought to—" Abruptly she stopped, staring at her daughter.

"What on earth are you doing, Lila?" she asked.

Lila paused, the piece of raw meat halfway to her mouth.

She had been about to eat it.

———

"Corey's not going to wait around for you much longer, you know," Samantha told Lila one afternoon over the phone. "He's got to get restless pretty soon, Li. When are you going to let him off the hook?"

"He's *off* the hook," Lila replied. "I let him off it. If I started going out with him again, that would be putting him back *on* the hook."

"Oh, don't get technical," Samantha said. "You know what I mean. When are you going to, you know, take pity on him?"

"And start going out with him again? Never."

"But you're being so mean!" Samantha wailed. "For no reason!"

"I have plenty of reasons," Lila said firmly. "I just can't explain them."

"Well, all I can say is they can't be such good reasons if you can't explain them. Come on, Lila. Marci's getting pissed. But don't tell her I told you that."

"Why's it any business of Marci's?" Lila asked a little angrily. "I haven't done anything to *her!*"

"Oh, she's not exactly mad at you," Samantha

soothed her. "She's just kind of bugged about you letting Karin Engals horn in like this. You know, Karin's really going after Corey—and she'll get him, too, if you don't stop her."

Lila laughed. "Has *anyone* ever stopped Karin Engals from doing anything she's ever wanted to do?"

"Well, you could have," Samantha said. "At least, the way you *used* to be, you could have."

"What do you mean, the way I used to be?" Lila snapped.

"You know," Samantha faltered, "before you got all . . . um, you know, moony."

Moony was the real problem, Lila knew. The full moon would arrive in just a few days. Would it happen? Was she going to transform again?

The signs were pretty clear that she would. Now that she was focusing inward so intently, Lila noticed countless little hints that her body was already preparing for the change. Her fingernails seemed thicker. She thought—or was that her imagination?—that she could see better in the dark. And her sense of smell was definitely sharper. Hearing her father tell off an employee over the phone, Lila could, without any doubt, smell the waves of anger that were emanating from him.

By the first day of the full moon, the scar on her leg had begun to fester again. Now Lila knew what was going to happen.

I'll go to bed extra-early, she promised herself after school. She was sitting by herself on the school bus, staring out the window. *Right after dinner. Kind of like an athlete in training. I have a long night ahead of me. I might as well catch up on my sleep. And I'll eat a really huge dinner. That way, when I'm outside, I won't be so tempted to—*

To kill something for food. But she wouldn't let herself finish the thought.

It was a bright, clear day, one of those days when the air looks as though it's been washed. Certainly there was no chance it would cloud over before dark.

Lila could hardly believe she'd be able to fall asleep, she was so nervous. But the preparations her body was making for the transformation must have been overwhelming. After supper, she slowly climbed the stairs to her room. Heart hammering in her chest, she undressed, put on a T-shirt, and pulled back her covers. Her body had scarcely touched the sheets before she fell into a black dreamless sleep.

Tonight, the forest is not big enough for her. It doesn't hold the one she's looking for. Not that she knows who that is. Before, her hunts have had more specific goals: rabbits, squirrels, other insignificant prey. Tonight her only clues about her quarry are that he is a male of her kind, and that he is much more powerful than she. Other than that, she doesn't even know what he smells like.

But she can tell that the forest is terrified of him. Anguished squeaks and squeals keep twittering out from the holes and burrows she passes. The little animals fear a daunting presence. Even the trees seem to have drawn together into watchful clusters. Tonight, the stream is hushed, as if listening. Tonight, the forest's dark caves almost eagerly throw their shadows open to the moon. *He is not coming here . . . not here,* the forest seems to whisper with every rustling branch. *We are safe. We are safe . . .*

Of course no one is safe. But the wolf can't resist running on. She must find him. She has no choice.

Running with her head down, the wolf finally catches his scent along a narrow trail. She recognizes it without knowing how. It's so complicated, the way her nose works. In captivity, she would be able to pick out this scent, even if it had been diluted by a thousand percent. Undiluted out here in the open, in the woods, it reaches her like wine pouring down her throat. It is sending her a signal she can't ignore: *Follow me.*

An owl screams a warning as the wolf's dark form lopes past. The wolf doesn't even hear.

He is just ahead, she tells herself breathlessly, . . . a little farther . . . a little farther . . .

Lila awoke, freezing and frightened, curled up in a ditch. Slowly, confusedly, she lifted her head and stretched her aching arms and legs. Where was she? This was a beautiful spot, but she didn't recognize it at all.

She seemed to be on a little dirt road out in the country. There were no buildings anywhere, just wet meadows and little clumps of pine trees and, in the distance, a hilly patchwork of fields and forests. The red sun was barely above the horizon. It was still so early in the morning that mist was rising from the grass.

Lila was shivering uncontrollably. The ditch was damp and stony, and her hands and feet were numb. Glancing down at her legs, she saw that they were again covered with telltale scratches. So she *had* become a wolf last night.

"And how am I going to get home?" she gasped aloud, stumbling to her feet. Then, as reality hit her, she slowly sank down again. Not only was she scratched and filthy—she was also naked.

Lila wanted to cry. This couldn't be happening. How could something so exactly like the most humiliating kind of nightmare be real?

I'll have to get help, she told herself frantically, hugging herself to keep warm. But how? What if someone drove by and saw her? What could she do?

Suddenly Lila froze. Someone *was* coming down the road. Her senses still heightened by the previous night's transformation, she recognized him long before she saw him.

It was the boy on the motorcycle.

Oh, my God, no. Not this. Not him.

The motorcycle was drawing inexorably closer.

Lila could not meet the eyes of its rider. She stared down at the ground, paralyzed with horror and embarrassment. The motorcycle was slowing now. And slowing even more . . . And stopping.

He was there. Next to her. Looking down at her.

"Please," Lila began to beg, looking up from the ground at her pursuer. "Please don't hurt—"

All speech left her at the sight of his face. She didn't know anything about him, but she could tell he wasn't here to hurt her.

He was staring down at her with a strange mixture of disappointment and pity in his green eyes. Slowly he extended a hand as if to help her to her feet. Then he seemed to think better of it. He shook his head and pulled his hand back. Reaching into a backpack strapped behind the motorcycle seat, he pulled out a rolled-up blanket and tossed it down to her.

"Wrap this around yourself," he said. His voice sounded rusty with disuse.

Silently, still staring mutely up at him, Lila obeyed. "Thank you," she tried to say, but her mouth wouldn't form the words.

The boy took a step toward Lila, who flinched nervously. Again a look of disappointment flashed across his face. He reached into the backpack, took out a pile of crumpled clothes, and dropped them in front of her.

"Look, I brought you some clothes, that's all," he said. "I don't expect you to trust me. Not yet."

His voice was rough, almost surly, but Lila somehow got the impression that he wished he could be nicer to her. It was only a fleeting impression, though, for the boy didn't say another word. He climbed back onto his motorcycle and started it with a roar.

"Wait!" Lila called. "How did you . . ." But he only continued on down the road without looking back.

"How did you know where I was?" Lila finished, in a whisper. "How did you know I'd need something to wear?

"What's going on?"

With shaking hands she spread the clothes out next to her. A faded pair of jeans, a torn sweatshirt, and a frayed denim jacket. No shoes, but a heavy pair of socks; she'd be able to manage in those for now. All of it was much too big for her—it must be his stuff—but everything was clean.

Quickly Lila dressed and rolled up the blanket. Then, her shivering gradually abating, she began to walk down the road.

There would have to be a house somewhere on this road. She'd call home from there.

How it happened

"And you say you found him in your barn?" the state trooper asked.

Mrs. Ramsey, a stout, capable-looking woman in her late forties, nodded vigorously. "The poor little thing must have been starving." She shuddered. "I found him with a dead hen in his hand. He'd bitten her through the throat, and he was eating her raw. Feathers and all. He's as skinny as—I cried when I first got him in here and saw what he really looked like."

"And he was wearing what he has on now?" The trooper glanced down at the small, black-haired boy sitting limply on the floor in the corner of Mrs. Ramsey's kitchen. He was about eight years old and dressed in clothes that must have fit him once. Now, where they weren't impossibly tight, they were pathetically shredded. His bare feet were so covered with ground-in dirt they might have been leather instead of skin.

"Well, I have other clothes he can wear," Mrs. Ramsey said defensively. "All the boys' stuff from when they were little. It's just, I thought you'd want to see him the way he was when I found him."

"Right." The trooper glanced at the boy and jotted a

few more notes on his pad. "Did he tell you his name?"

"He didn't tell me anything."

"You mean he can't talk?" the trooper asked.

"Doesn't seem to. I've tried, but he just kind of ignores me."

Indeed, the child was paying them no attention at all. He was examining his hands, carefully turning them over and over as if they held some secret. At last, with a kind of hopeless exhaustion, he let them dangle at his sides.

"He screamed like a wild thing when I found him in the barn. Then he collapsed at my feet."

"Do you think he's deaf?" asked the trooper.

"No, he can hear. He just doesn't seem to care what he's hearing. Watch." Mrs. Ramsey banged a saucepan lid on her spotless stove. The boy blinked when he heard the clang, but otherwise he didn't move.

"Defective, maybe," the trooper suggested.

"Well, he's got a fever. That might account for it." Mrs. Ramsey sighed. "Who'd do something to a poor little boy like this? Leaving him out in the woods to fend for himself? He's been out there for days, by the looks of him!"

There was no way she could know it had actually been two and a half years, or that no abandonment could have seemed worse to the boy himself than the terror he'd been freed of—or than to be caught this way.

"It's a pity." The trooper was silent for a minute, watching the child. The boy's unearthly stillness made him uneasy. He cleared his throat loudly and said, "Well, thanks for calling me, Mrs. Ramsey. I'll take him along now and keep you posted."

"Take him?" Mrs. Ramsey looked startled. "Take him where?"

"I've got to let the county know about him so they can evaluate him. Then they'll decide the best place for him."

"Why can't I keep him? I found him!" the woman protested.

"Well, now, this isn't finders keepers we're playing here. The county'll have to decide. If you really want to keep him—"

"Of course I do! Poor little thing! It's not as though we don't have the room! My boys are on their own now."

"I'm sure the county will take your wishes into consideration." The trooper sighed. He, too, wished he could just leave the little boy here. Surely he would be worse off *being dragged through all the paperwork that awaited the two of them. And then the boy'd have to go into the hospital for observation, probably, and God only knew what would happen after that. Whereas Mrs. Ramsey, the trooper knew, would feed him and bathe him and put him into a warm bed and generally act like the mother hen she was. And wouldn't that be better for everyone?*

But that wasn't the way these agencies worked. Everyone did the best they could, and did it all wrong. Maybe she'd get him back after all, though. It had happened before.

The trooper walked over to the boy and tapped him gently on the shoulder. "Come on, guy," he said. "Time to go for a little ride. We're going to get you all fixed up, you'll see."

The child didn't move.

The trooper sighed. Then, bending over, he lifted the boy into his arms. He was shocked at how little he weighed. Like carrying a crumpled paper bag. And Mrs. Ramsey was right. The boy's stick body was terribly hot.

"I'll keep you posted," the trooper said again.

"Do that. Please." Mrs. Ramsey blew her nose. Then she patted the boy's head and looked into his startlingly green eyes. For a second he returned her gaze. Then his

eyes slid away. He looked, she thought, as though he were already dead.

"You take care of yourself now," Mrs. Ramsey said steadily. "I'll be thinking about you."

She never saw him again.

CHAPTER 12

"Are we slowing down a little in our old age, Lila?" Karin Engals asked witchily. She was standing in the girls' locker room next to Lila, who was wearily changing out of her gym clothes. "What was it— three hours late to school? And now you can't even get dressed."

"Give it a rest, Karin," Lila said tiredly. She pulled off a sneaker and threw it into her locker. "We all have our off days."

"It's just that you've had so *many* of them lately," Karin cooed. "You're not pregnant, are you?"

Lila looked at her in amazement. "What did you say?"

"Well, you're sure acting it," Karin said with a shrug. "Feeling sick in the mornings?" she asked mock-solicitously. "Is that why we've been coming in late? Can't eat?—I watched you at lunch. Shadows under the new mother's eyes?"

"Don't be ridiculous," Lila snapped, and instantly regretted it.

"And look! She's extra-emotional, too," Karin continued. "Hormonal changes, I guess. I *thought* there had to be some reason you and Corey were acting so weird before you broke up."

Lila glanced at the two senior girls who were a few feet down the row of lockers. They were busily changing their clothes, but the fact that they'd fallen completely silent made her sure they were listening just as busily.

She forced a laugh. "Well, Karin, all I can tell you is that if I *were* pregnant, it would be a miracle. How are *you* making out with Corey?" she added sweetly.

Karin's answer was equally sweet. "Great! I don't think he even remembers your name anymore."

"You keep working on him, and I'm sure he'll forget everything he knows." *I don't really know what I mean by that,* Lila added silently, *but on the other hand you don't, either.* She closed her locker door carefully. She didn't want to give the slightest impression that she was slamming it. "See you next period."

Feeling mildly triumphant, she headed for the locker-room door. But when she stopped to check her hair in the mirror, the feeling evaporated.

Behind her reflection she could see the two seniors who'd overheard her conversation with Karin. They were eyeing her in the mirror, and one was whispering, half-smiling, to the other. When they caught Lila's gaze, they turned away immediately.

I don't care, Lila told herself, lifting her chin. *They can all go right to hell.*

But it was hard not to care. It had taken the simplest thing, a full moon, to strip away most of the life she'd known. Could the moon offer her anything in return?

Please, Lila prayed silently. *Please, if you have to wreck everything in my* real *life, then at least give me something to make up for it.*

"I suppose we'll have to lock your door," Mrs. Crawford said that night after supper. She leaned into Lila's room and frowned down at her daughter, who was doing her homework. "We can't have you wandering around loose at night."

Lila smiled weakly. " 'Loose'? That's a funny way of putting it."

"Well, it *applies* in this case," her mother told her. "I'm going to lock the doors and windows both. If you're going to sleepwalk, you can confine it to your bedroom. You just let me know when you're ready."

"Are you planning to unlock the doors in the morning?" Lila asked. "Or are you just going to wall me up in here for the rest of my life, like Mrs. Rochester in *Jane Eyre?*"

"Don't be silly, Lila. Certainly we'll let you out. You've got school, don't forget."

Although considering the way Karin is gunning for me at school, I may be safer here.

Of course Mrs. Crawford can't know that once Lila has transformed, she doesn't need to have the windows unlocked—or even open. All she has to do is think about being outside, and she's there. Which is exactly what happens the instant the moon is high enough in the sky that night.

Once out on the street, the wolf heads for the woods right away. Tonight she retains enough of her human memory to be wary about going too far. It will have to be the forest only, none of the fields beyond. She needs to know she can get back safely before the sun rises. If the other one is not in the woods, then she'll have to be on her own tonight.

But he is actually standing at the edge of the forest when she gets there.

Amazed, she stops short. She stares at him for a long moment, sniffing the air. Then, her eyes locked on his, she stalks straight-legged toward him.

He is a huge black wolf. She has never seen another wolf; she does not even know what she looks like; but all the same she recognizes him as a version of herself. A more impressive version, certainly. Older. Easily twice her size. Green eyes. Front paws the size of saucers. He is not moving at all, and hardly breathing. She recognizes his stance: This is how he waits for prey.

She whimpers a little in surprise. Doesn't he recognize *her*?

Then the male lowers his head slightly, as if nodding at her. *Approach, but beware.*

Like all the canids, wolves use body language to send a vast range of signals to one another. Placement of the head, the shoulders, the tail are all crucial indicators of mood. Each member of a wolf pack moves in ways that instantly announce his rank to his companions. Here there is no pack to tell the female where this male stands in relation to her. So as she approaches him, her own posture must strike a balance between attack and flight. She wants to show respect, but not deference; wariness, but not fear.

The male stands perfectly still. He, at any rate, is not going to change his posture until she is closer. . . .

It's all up to her. She walks up to him, breathing hard, until they are almost nose to nose. Then she lowers her head almost to the ground.

The male considers this. He tilts his own head to one side. For a few seconds, the two of them stand there frozen in their poses. Then, very gently, the male slides his right front paw forward until it touches the female's.

It's not a conventional wolf gesture. But then, these two are not purebreds. For werewolves, there might be a few variations in the rules.

Certainly the joy that courses through the female at the male's touch would seem to be more human than animal. At last, at *last*, she has found what she was looking for.

It is hours before the two finally begin to tire. They have raced through the woods together for miles, their muscles rippling in unison—a perfectly matched team, except for size. Once again the female might have forgotten the time, but as the night sky lightens to a dark gray, her companion slows down. When she too stops running, the female suddenly realizes how late it is—and how hungry she is.

She glances over and realizes the other wolf is as hungry as she.

Of course it is much easier for two wolves to hunt together than separately. That, too, is part of pack life. So the two of them hardly need to exchange more than a glance when they catch the scent of the first deer to wake in the woods on that early, early morning.

He is a five-point buck, so used to walking un-challenged that it never occurs to him to go quietly. By the time he catches their scent, it is much too late.

The wolves are both bloody when they finally lift their heads from the kill. To the female's dismay, the gray sky has lightened to lavender. She hasn't thought about the sunrise at all, and now it is al-most upon her.

She eyes her companion with dismay. Where can they go? Can he come with her?

No, he tells her. *You have to go alone.* He nudges her shoulder gently. The sky is pink now.

But I don't want to go, she answers.

The male nudges her again. *We have no choice.*

Tomorrow night, then?

Tomorrow night.

She looks at him for a second longer, and then begins to run toward the houses.

When Lila vaulted into her bedroom and turned back into herself, she realized three things. First, there were smears of blood all over her body.

Second, her alarm clock was about to ring. She sprang forward to shut it off before it could waken her parents.

And finally, she remembered that her bedroom door was locked from the outside.

Next time I'll think myself back into the bathroom, just in case, she thought dreamily. Being blood-stained was only a technicality this morning. *Let's see, I'll lie under the covers until Mom and Dad unlock the door, and then I'll wait until they're downstairs before I head to the shower. It'll be easy.*

Lila smiled as she snuggled down into bed and pulled the covers over her head. Everything was going to be easy from now on. There wouldn't be any more obstacles, none that mattered, anyway. School wasn't important. Her friends were trivial. Her parents meant nothing at all. She had found what she was looking for, and the rest of life was just a matter of passing the time until she could be with him again.

At least that was what she thought until the third night.

CHAPTER 13

My love, does it not grieve you
That I so wretched be?
Then hold me in your arms, dear,
Let winter fly from me . . .

It was two-thirty in the afternoon, and Lila was singing along with the rest of the Pelham High School Senior Choir. Along with the rest of the choir, too, she was wondering exactly how Mr. Dunkel, the music teacher, managed to look so much like a monkey when he conducted. Dunkel the Monkel, everyone called him. Really, it was incredible. A beautiful song like this, and Mr. Dunkel was leaping around the music room flapping his arms as if he were trying to ruin it on purpose.

She didn't mind Mr. Dunkel, of course. This was

a lot better than the times they sang semi-hip songs and Mr. Dunkel favored them with his own special version of dancing. Besides, Lila couldn't mind anything today. She was floating giddily above the whole world, waiting for night and the moon. At the thought of what the moon would bring her tonight, she flashed a smile of such radiant happiness that Karin Engals, who was singing across the room from her, stared at her in astonishment.

"Then hold me in your arms, dear, / Let winter fly from me," the choir finished on a note of muted triumph.

"Perfect! Perfect!" Mr. Dunkel ceased his leaps and leaned against the piano in the middle of the room. "That was great, guys. I don't think we need to do it again. You've really got it down. You're gonna knock 'em dead tonight."

"Knock *who* dead?" Lila whispered to the girl standing next to her.

"The audience, duh," the girl answered, furtively transferring a wad of gum from one side of her cheek to the other.

"What audience?"

"The *concert* audience. Where have you been for

the past six weeks? We've been rehearsing for the All-School Concert tonight, remember? In the auditorium?"

"Oh, right," Lila answered sheepishly. "I guess I was thinking about . . . something else." She finished in horror: "Wait a minute! I can't come tonight!"

"Don't tell *me* about it," said the bored girl next to her. "Tell the Monkel. But I think you've passed the deadline. Didn't he say all the excuses had to be in by last week?"

Yes. That was what he had said, as Lila found out when she approached him after rehearsal.

"Lila, I'm disappointed in you," Mr. Dunkel told her, shaking his head. "You've never tried to bag out on me before. You know what our rule is."

"Yes, but—"

"We depend on one another in Senior Choir. Choir is an elective course, but once you commit to it, you *commit* to it. That means you can't get out of concerts without giving me proper notice. And telling me on the day of the concert is certainly not proper notice."

"But Mr. Dunkel, it's really impor—"

"The concert is more important. I'll see you there," her teacher interrupted.

"Okay," Lila answered weakly. "But do you know when it will be over? Because there's someplace I've really, really got to be afterward."

Mr. Dunkel regarded her impatiently. "Well, I haven't *timed* it. I should think it will take the same amount of time our concerts usually take, about two hours. As you should know very well, Lila. This is your third All-School Concert, isn't it?"

But it's the first where I might actually change into a wolf onstage, Lila thought in despair. Dejectedly she decided that the only thing she'd be able to do would be to skip the concert and plan on getting into trouble later.

Unfortunately, she didn't even get the chance to do that. At supper that night, her mother announced that she and Mr. Crawford had decided to go to the concert. "We missed last year's," she said, "and we both agree that it's important to support culture in the schools. We'll drive you there."

"And back, of course," said Lila's father with a dry little chuckle.

Of course. They weren't going to leave her any

escape route at all. From seven-thirty until at least nine-thirty, Lila was stuck inside the school building, where everyone could see her. All she could hope was that she wouldn't transform until after that.

The scar on Lila's leg started to pulse just after the ninth-graders began singing old Civil War ballads. It began actively throbbing when the sophomores started in on their collection of Broadway medleys. "Stop *fidgeting*," Mrs. Crawford hissed irritably after Lila had leaned over to check her leg for the third time.

But it was impossible to sit still when her skin was crawling like this. The scar was literally getting hot, Lila noticed worriedly. She didn't think that had happened before. Was it a sign that she was going to transform earlier than usual this evening?

There was a sudden crash of applause, and Lila jerked back to the present. Were the sophomores done already? They had to be, she guessed; they were filing back to their seats. A beaming, sweating Mr. Dunkel turned to the audience.

"Weren't they great?" he shouted over the applause. "Let's give them a big hand!"

Why do people always say that? Lila wondered. *It only makes the clapping wind down instead of—*But Mr. Dunkel was speaking again.

"I'd like to announce a short intermission before our Senior Choir performs," he said. "Choir, please meet me backstage in ten minutes."

Thank you, thank you, thought Lila gratefully, jumping to her feet. At least she'd be able to get out of this cramped auditorium seat for a while. She turned to her parents.

"I think I'll get up and stretch my legs," she told them politely. *Before they explode.* "Would either of you like anything? There's juice and stuff out in the lobby."

But both the Crawfords were already pulling out work from the briefcases they'd brought with them for just this kind of emergency. "No, thanks, dear," said Mrs. Crawford absently. "Maybe after the concert, though."

"Fine. See you later." Lila squirmed her way past a row of knees and coats and headed out to the front hall. It was a little less cramped there, but still

. . . Without conscious thought she walked to the front door and pushed it open.

Instant relief. Blessedly icy air streamed over her face, cooling her burning skin and bringing her back to herself. The moon was nowhere in sight yet, Lila saw. In maybe forty-five more minutes she'd be able to escape from all this turmoil and—

"Hey! What're you trying to do, freeze us to death?" someone shouted from behind her. "Close that door!"

"Sorry," Lila called back over her shoulder, and stepped out onto the front steps alone.

Outside, the night was even better. The wind was so strong Lila could hardly stand upright against it. The bare silhouettes of trees were whipping back and forth against the sky, and hundreds of dead leaves were skittering along the sidewalk like tiny dried-out ghosts. *This is perfect*, Lila thought gratefully, holding her face up to the wind. *This is exactly what I needed.*

"Well, look at our nature girl communing with the heavens," came a drawling voice from around the corner of the school.

"Karin." Lila didn't have to turn around to know

who was talking. She leaned against the wall of the school resignedly. Karin Engals strolled over, a lit cigarette in one hand.

"Want one?" she asked. "Oh, no. I forgot you're not-smoking for two."

"That whole routine is getting kind of boring, you know," said Lila as cheerfully as she could manage. "You're working it to death. You should get a little more variety into your act. Isn't there some other way you could pick on me? You know— rig my locker or steal my friends or something?"

"You don't really have many friends left, or haven't you noticed?" Karin blew an expressive plume of smoke straight into Lila's face. "And speaking of acts, *you* shouldn't try to steal mine. I mean, stop acting all casual with me. It doesn't work. You're not good at pretending you don't care about things. I'd believe you a lot more easily if you'd stamp your feet and cry."

"Why should I? I'm really not that upset," said Lila serenely. *At least not tonight. At least now that I have something to look forward to.*

"Really? Not with Mr. Motorcycle to keep you company, I guess. Your little imaginary friend."

Lila spun around to face the other girl. "Where did you hear about him?" she gasped before she could stop herself. *Who betrayed me?*

"Where do you think?" Karin exhaled another plume of smoke. "From Marci and Samantha."

"*They* told you? Not that there's anything to tell," Lila added hastily.

"I know there isn't. There *certainly* isn't. When are you going to introduce us all to him?" Karin asked tauntingly. "When are you going to meet him yourself? Don't you think it's kind of pathetic to be fainting around after someone you've never even said hi to?"

The moon was rising. Lila could feel it. Its force was building up inside her like evil champagne.

"You'd better go back inside, Karin," she said in a low voice. "I mean it."

"Oooh! So dramatic!" said Karin with a giggle. "What happens if I stay? Do we have a catfight?"

Lila couldn't answer. The change was upon her, and it was happening too fast.

Her palms. Her nails. Her skin. Her jaw.

Her skeleton was mutating. A tail appeared.

"What is your *problem?*" Karin asked. "You're looking really weird, I hate to tell you."

. Lila opened her mouth to explain, but only a snarl came out. She felt her teeth growing, sharpening. She dropped to her knees. Swiftly her leg joints rearranged themselves.

"Oh, no," Karin whispered. "No. No. No. No."

With her last second of human sight, Lila saw fear burst into flower on Karin's face. With her last second of human consciousness, she felt an incredible rush of satisfaction. *Now do you think I'm acting too casual?*

Karin, too, dropped to her knees, but it was only to pray.

"Please, Lila. Whoever you are. Please go away," she begged insanely. "I-I never meant to—"

Now Lila's eyes had changed, too, and all she saw was the enemy standing in front of her.

Who is this tormenter? Why is it blocking my path like this? she asks herself. The human is a shaking, trembling blob on the ground before her, but the wolf doesn't waste any time on pity.

She gathers her strength and lunges forward, aiming right for the throat.

What began as Karin's scream turns into a sickening gurgle. The wolf grabs her by the neck and shakes her hard.

Somewhere a door bursts open, dropping a long rectangle of light onto the lawn.

"Anybody out here? It's time to—Hey, what's happening?" a familiar voice shouts hoarsely. "Oh, my God! *Help!* Somebody get help!"

People pour out the door in a jumble of noise.

In a flash the wolf vanishes. Karin—her eyes lolling whitely, her throat gaping, ripped open—rolls down the front steps and lies motionless at the bottom.

Two Wolves

He is standing in the same place where he stood last night. Once again, he waits motionless as she approaches.

They do not use words to communicate. Somehow each knows what the other is thinking. They send a series of images and emotions back and forth in a silent language neither knew until they met.

Trouble? *he asks when she is close enough for him to see the blood drenching the front half of her body.*

Terrible trouble. *Quickly the female sends him the image of what she has just done. As he absorbs the story, his body grows tense.*

I'm sorry, *she falters, sensing his unease.*

Too late for that, *he answers somewhat wearily.* But I had hoped for more time. . . . *The male thinks for a second.* Follow me, *he finally says.*

He leads her to the stream and plunges in. After a second, she does the same. The icy water hits her like a knife, but after a second she's grateful to it. You can't feel any emotions when you're fighting off such cold.

As the stream courses over her, rinsing away the blood, the female begins to care less and less about what she's just been through. It's over. She couldn't help it. And in the meantime, she's here. That troubled other world doesn't seem real now. Why not put it out of her mind?

Which is just what she does for the rest of the night. The forest is so beautiful, and so untainted.

Unfortunately, morning always comes, whether you want it to or not.

CHAPTER 14

The sun was just slipping into view when Lila rematerialized in her bedroom in human form. Immediately she noticed that the house seemed strangely busy for that hour of the morning. Already there was the smell of coffee brewing, and the sound of footsteps walking rapidly downstairs. Tiptoeing to her door, Lila opened it a crack and heard a strange woman's voice talking on the phone downstairs. She walked softly to the window and peered outside. There was a police car parked in front of the house.

"What's that for?" Lila muttered distractedly. Why would there be police at *her* house? Could they know? How?

Then she realized what must be going on, and sat limply down on her bed in dismay. They were looking for her. Not for the wolf—for her, Lila. She hadn't been home all night.

How am I going to explain this? For the second time?

Thank heaven she wasn't covered with blood *this* morning. It was going to be tough enough to explain everything else. Like, for example, how she had gotten upstairs to her room without anyone seeing her.

Oh, God, she was so tired. She would never be able to come up with a decent story, and yet she had no choice, really, because who would believe her if she told the truth?

She couldn't hide up here for much longer, anyway. It would only be putting off the inevitable. She had to think of something right now.

I'll bluff it, she thought grimly. *I have nothing to lose.*

Lila pushed her door open and walked resolutely into the hall. "Mom?" she called down the stairs. "Where are you?"

"Lila!" Her mother dashed up the stairs and gripped her daughter fiercely by the shoulders. "Where on *earth* have you been?" she asked furiously. "We've been looking for you all night!" She called to someone over her shoulder. "It's all right. She's here."

In a second a police officer—a young woman with curly red hair—and Lila's father had joined Mrs. Crawford at the foot of the stairs. *Here comes the bride,* thought Lila idiotically as she stared down at their upturned faces. *My one chance to make a big entrance, and I forget my lines.*

"Well, young lady?" said her father sternly. "What's your explanation for putting us through this agony?"

"I'll tell you." Lila's voice was faint. "But Mom, please let go. You're hurting me."

"Let's all go into the kitchen," suggested the officer authoritatively. "I'll just call in to the station and let them know she's here, and then she can fill us in."

Once they were all in the kitchen, Lila collapsed into a chair. It wasn't an act. She could hardly stand. Her mother appeared unmoved, however. Leaning against the counter, she crossed her arms and gave Lila her best I'm-waiting-for-this glare.

"I've already told Sergeant Gioia you pulled this

stunt last month," she said crossly. "So don't act as though it's the first time."

"It's not like that, Mom." Obviously she was going to have to lie her way out of this. Still, she'd probably do best to stick as close to the truth as she could. "You heard about what happened to Karin Engals?"

"Of course we did. We were there," her father reminded her. "Why do you think we called the police?"

Lila leaned her head on her hands. "Mom, I *saw* what happened to her."

Sergeant Gioia leaned forward quickly. "You saw the attack?" she asked.

Lila shuddered. Again, it wasn't an act. "Yes, I did. I had just gone out to get some air. It was so stuffy in the school. I saw her walking around smoking a cigarette by herself." Her chin was trembling uncontrollably. Even the doctored version of the story was terrible to think about. "We started talking. And while we were standing there, this dog came out at us from around the side of the building. A big dog. Like a husky or something. I couldn't see it too well. I thought it was Karin's dog, maybe.

"But it obviously wasn't," she went on. "It kind of leaped on her. And Karin screamed, and fell, and . . . and there was so much blood all over the place. And the dog started shaking her by the neck."

Lila put her head in her hands. "And then it went for me," she said.

"The dog attacked you?" asked the officer.

"It wanted to, but it didn't touch me," Lila said quickly. This time around, she didn't want anyone asking why she *wasn't* bloody. "I ran away just in time. The dog kept on after me."

"Why didn't you scream?" asked the officer.

Lila's eyes widened. "I did! I screamed like crazy! But no one heard me, I guess. By then, I was way out on the football field."

"That's entirely possible, in all the crowd," her father said grudgingly. He turned to Mrs. Crawford. "You know how hard it was to find anyone what with all those hysterical types milling around outside. That's why we thought Lila must have gone home," he told Sergeant Gioia.

"I wanted to go home," Lila lied. "But the dog

wouldn't stop chasing me. Finally I came to this tree I could climb."

"You were still on the football field?" asked the officer skeptically.

"Oh, no, no. I don't really know where I was by then. Coming into a neighborhood, I think. Like maybe over near Oakdale Drive?" Lila said tentatively.

"And you didn't see anyone?" the officer asked.

"Well, I wasn't . . . I wasn't *near* any of the houses." *Please don't let this story fall apart,* Lila prayed. "I was sort of just coming up on their backyards. Anyway, so I climbed this tree as fast as I could." Lila held out her hands. "You can see where it scratched me. And the dog just stayed down there, waiting for me. I don't know how long it was. I couldn't see my watch. But finally it walked away.

"I didn't dare come down, though," Lila continued. "I stayed up there for maybe another hour. In case it was waiting for me somewhere nearby. And then when it finally started to get a little bit lighter, I climbed down and headed for home. . . . And here I am," she finished warily.

Was it going to work? Lila realized with a pang that Sergeant Gioia was still looking doubtful. "But you came from upstairs," she said slowly.

Uh-oh. There was only one thing to say, and it was pretty feeble. "I climbed in through my bedroom window. I didn't want to worry my parents."

"Didn't want to *worry* us!" her mother exclaimed incredulously. "What are you talking about, Lila? Why, we were already worried sick! And why wouldn't it worry us to have you climb through the window, for heaven's sake?"

"I guess I wasn't thinking very clearly, Mom." Lila's voice cracked. "I really don't want to talk anymore. I'm awfully tired, and school will be starting soon. Can't I please just go take a shower and change my clothes?"

Mrs. Crawford glanced at Sergeant Gioia. After a second, the officer nodded.

The look she gave Lila was a lot more searching than Lila would have liked.

"How's Karin?" Lila asked quickly. "Is there any news?"

Sergeant Gioia was silent for a minute. "There's news, yes. She's probably not going to make it."

———

Lila was standing in the shower under the hottest water she could stand. The spray felt as though it was peeling her skin off, but it still wasn't enough. It would never wash away the blood this time. Even if every bit of Lila's body was washed away, nothing would ever get rid of *this* blood.

I attacked a human last night. A person. For no reason. I truly am a monster.

Lila tried to console herself by remembering how Karin had goaded her, but it didn't do any good. You didn't rip peoples' throats out just because they were hateful!

Just having Karin see you change into a wolf would have been scary enough for her, Lila told herself bitterly. *You didn't have to go all the way.*

But could she have controlled herself once the transformation had started? Lila didn't think so. It had all happened so fast that there hadn't been *time* to run away. Maybe her rage at Karin had speeded things up, though. Maybe if she'd managed to stay calmer, she'd have been able to get out of sight before she changed.

Maybe it was her fault, and maybe it wasn't. But

what was the use of trying to decide? It wouldn't make any difference to Karin.

It was the first time Lila could remember walking into a totally silent school. So the word was out, then.

No one was moving. People huddled in frightened-looking clumps along the rows of lockers, speaking in whispers. Now and then a teacher would walk to a classroom door and peer out into the hall, but that was all. The principal had probably told them to go easy on the kids this morning.

Maybe they'll even give us those trauma-counseling sessions kids on the TV news get when a sniper or something attacks their school. Boy, I should be first in line.

It seemed to Lila that her footsteps were much too loud. She thought everyone turned and stared at her as she walked down the hall, but that had to be her imagination. No one could possibly connect *her* with what had happened to Karin, could they?

Could they?

Lila continued down the hall under those watchful eyes. Her locker seemed much too far away. The corridor was endless. She felt as though she were walking underwater—slowly, falteringly—to reach it.

When she finally got there, Marci and Samantha were waiting for her.

"Hey, nice to see you again," Lila said automatically. "How are you?"

Samantha didn't even bother answering the question. "You heard, right?" she whispered eagerly. She was as peppy as ever, Lila noticed dryly. This might be bad news, but there are some people who live to spread bad news. "That Karin's not expected to live?"

"I heard." Lila opened her locker door without seeing it, her mind racing. *Am I a murderer if she dies?*

"Corey's really, really upset," Marci said. "We ran into him this morning. He was driving to the hospital to see her. He's the one who found her, you know."

"No, I-I didn't know that." It took a terrible effort to get the words out.

"She was talking when he found her, he said. Babbling, kind of."

"What did she say?" Lila asked in alarm.

"Something about being attacked, I guess. He told us none of it made any sense," Marci told her.

"He said she sounded crazy," Samantha said. "She must've been so scared she lost her mind. Corey was pretty freaked out. He thinks that even if she lives, she'll never be normal again."

"And he told us to give you a message," Marci put in.

"A message," Lila repeated dully. What now?

"He has to talk to you." Samantha's eyes were bright with curiosity and suspicion. "He says it's important."

The New Patient

People sometimes joke about the Bancroft Psychiatric Facility. It would be so much easier to take if it didn't look so much like a . . . well, an old-fashioned lunatic asylum. The place is a dark-red Victorian monstrosity. Tiny barred windows, steep pointed dormers, a massive front door with an iron ring for a knocker—the works. You half-expect, on walking up the narrow front path (brick, of course) to hear organ music and piercing shrieks wafting down from the top floor. When people pass the sharp-pointed iron fence that runs the length of the property, they can't help shuddering. Then they laugh at themselves half-heartedly.

Inside, though, everything is fine. It's all perfectly up-to-date and clean. This isn't the snake pit, you realize with a sigh of relief as you step inside. It's just a hospital.

Someone new has arrived at Bancroft today. That's her room down the hall there. The closed door with the little window in the center. You can look in, if you like. You won't disturb her. In fact, she won't even know you're there.

She's about sixteen, with a face that's too thin and

sharp for real prettiness. Her throat is heavily bandaged, which is just as well; the scars underneath are rather . . . distinctive. Not to her, of course. She's not aware that she has them.

The girl is so quiet, lying there on her bed in the dim room, that at first you might think she's sleeping. But her eyes are open, and staring at the ceiling with a fixed look of terror. And her lips are moving. They never stop moving, never stop their ceaseless whispered entreaties.

She's not a very appealing person, it's true. If you had known her before this happened to her, you might not have liked her. But even her worst enemies would agree that she's been punished enough. No one that young should be so terrified. So permanently *terrified.*

Most of the residents at Bancroft get better. Most of them get to go home and start over again. But not Karin Engals.

Karin is never going home.

CHAPTER 15

"Lila!"

Lila was walking through a department store, idly checking a price tag, when she heard him coming up behind her. She turned with a sinking heart and saw Corey Ryan.

"Hi, Corey," she said with a wan smile. "Where'd you come from?"

"Didn't you hear me?" he asked. "Geez, I called you about five hundred times! I thought you'd just keep going forever and never turn around."

Good call, Lila wanted to say. These days, about the only way she could take her mind off things was to walk and walk and walk until she tired herself out. Today was Saturday. She had come downtown in the hopes that she'd find more to distract herself. Just walking around the block at home over and over wasn't doing the trick.

"Well, I'm glad I spotted you," Corey was saying. "Why didn't you call me back, Lila?"

He had called a dozen times over the past two days. And every time he'd called, Lila had asked her mother to say she would call back later.

"I've had a lot on my mind," Lila said evasively. She stared down at the glass counter in front of her. It was piled with leather gloves, sixty percent off. She didn't need any.

"Do you have time for coffee or something?" Corey asked. "I really have to talk to you."

"About *what*?" Lila said, trying to sound impatient. Her heart was thudding with dread, but she couldn't let Corey see that. "Haven't we talked enough already? What *more* do we have to talk about?"

"About Karin," said Corey.

Lila's stomach lurched. *He knows!* she thought, fighting for breath. *He's tracked me down!*

Then: *No, no, he couldn't know. He didn't see anything. He has no reason to guess I'm involved. Just keep calm.*

And stay mad. It was a good way to disguise fear.

"What *about* Karin?" Lila asked coldly. "You've

got a lot of nerve talking about your new girlfriend to your old one." The saleswoman behind the glove counter was watching them curiously, Lila saw. *We're putting on quite a soap opera for her,* she thought. *Maybe, if I try to look as if I'm shoplifting, she'll kick me out of the store and I won't have to go through with this.*

Unfortunately, the saleswoman simply continued to watch the show without interfering. But Corey was starting to look tense.

"Lila," he began wearily, "this has nothing to do with us. She's asking for you."

Oh, no. "For me? Why would she want to see me?"

"God knows," said Corey simply. "She just wants to see you. It's about the only un-mixed-up thing she's said since she was attacked, and I think it's the least you can do for her."

Lila relaxed a little. Corey obviously didn't know what had happened. He wouldn't have been able to hide it if he'd known. If she could just keep up her end of the conversation, she'd be fine. Pretending to be angry seemed to be working okay. All Lila cared about any longer was not giving herself away.

"Why should I want to do *anything* for Karin Engals?" she asked, sticking her chin into the air. "It's not as if I owe her something. We never even liked each other!"

"I know, but—Lila, she's really lost her mind." Corey looked as if it hurt to have to say something so final out loud. "They don't expect her ever to get better, you know."

Lila snorted. "That's really flattering. She wants to see me because she's lost her mind. Thanks a lot."

"Now, you know that's not what I—Hey, where are you going?"

"I'm leaving," Lila shot back over her shoulder as she walked swiftly toward the door. "You can find someone else to insult."

"Lila, that's *not* what I—Damn it, come back here!"

But Lila was gone.

I'm safe, she thought as she boarded the bus that would take her home. *I'm really safe.*

If Corey didn't suspect anything, then no one

would. And even if Karin became coherent enough to tell the truth, who'd believe her? A girl in a psychiatric hospital who said she'd been attacked by a werewolf?

"Yeah, right," Lila said under her breath. She was shaking with relief. Her secret would never need to come out.

And now all I have to do is put this behind me.

All of it. The transformations, the dreams, the— Lila set her jaw resolutely—the boy on the motorcycle. She had flown too close to an evil sun, and she had been scorched. She had to pull back now, or she'd burn up completely.

Pulling back was the only way to keep the truth hidden, she knew. No one would ever guess as long as Lila kept her secret self roped in. This was her chance to return to the safe, secure life she'd known before all this stuff had started happening. But it all depended on her keeping herself within bounds.

If I can just start acting like the old Lila again . . . If I just swear never to give in to my wolf side again . . . If I can just try hard enough!

It had to work. It had to.

But would it be enough for her, going back to the tame old life she'd lived before?

Lila slammed the door shut on that question. She wasn't going to let herself think about that kind of thing anymore. It would *have* to be enough. Better a dull, ordinary life than one so dramatic you caused tragedies every time you turned around. She might as well try to be mature about this. Passion was just too much of a risk.

The bus was almost at her stop before she heard the familiar purring of a motorcycle coming up alongside.

Lila closed her eyes and tried to steady her breath, which had suddenly gone all ragged. No. No. This was the one thing she couldn't let herself think about if she wanted everything to work out!

I'm going to be a regular person again, she reminded herself. *Marci and Samantha were right. There's no reason for me to get all excited about a guy I don't even know.*

"I'm not even going to look out the window," she muttered through clenched teeth. "So you can just forget about me."

The motorcycle drew up to her window and stayed there.

Lila tried. She really did. And when she finally gave up and glanced out the window, she saw that he was just outside the bus. He was riding along exactly parallel to her window, like a police escort.

Once he looked up into Lila's face as though reminding her of something. Like a child, she slid down into her seat so she wouldn't have to see him. When she looked up again, he was gone.

Lila tried to ignore how flat and empty she felt after that.

As the time for her next transformation drew closer, Lila began to make her plans. This time the moon wasn't going to get her. This time, she was going to stay herself. And if something went wrong and she transformed anyway—well, she wouldn't be able to get out of the house. She wouldn't be able to hurt anyone. Except herself.

"Lila, it turns out that both your father and I need to be away for a few days next week," Mrs. Crawford said one afternoon. She pointed to her desk calendar. "See, right here. We're both leaving on Tuesday and coming back on Saturday. Would you like me to arrange for someone to stay with you?"

"Stay with me?" Lila repeated. "Mom, I'm sixteen! I'll be fine."

"Make sure you take care of yourself, then," her mother said. "I certainly don't want to come home and hear that anything went on in this house that shouldn't have."

"I promise, Mom," Lila said solemnly. *I plan to make sure* no one *hears about it. And you couldn't possibly have picked a better time to take a trip.*

Her transformation would take place during the time her parents were gone.

"Now, let's see," Lila murmured to herself as she paced restlessly around her room. It was almost six-thirty at night. The full moon would be starting to rise in a few minutes.

"Window blinds." Lila pulled them down and then, for good measure, covered them with towels. That should keep the poisonous moonlight away from her.

"Pill," she went on, tiptoeing nervously across the hall and into her mother's bathroom.

As she constantly liked to remind people, Mrs. Crawford had a hard time falling asleep. Six months before, she had finally badgered her doctor into prescribing sleeping pills for her, which then gave her the opportunity to complain about how hard it was to wake up in the morning after she'd taken a pill. This complaint must have had some basis in fact, though, since Mrs. Crawford had soon stopped taking the pills and gone back to complaining about not getting enough sleep. Ever since then, the pills had been sitting in the bathroom medicine cabinet.

I'm not stealing drugs, Lila reminded herself as she nervously opened the medicine cabinet. *I'm just borrowing one sleeping pill so I can stay at home and not cause any trouble. If this isn't a true medicinal need, then I don't know what is. If Mom knew the truth—as if anyone could believe the truth—she'd approve.*

She carried the pill into her own room and put it next to her bed along with a glass of water. There was still one thing she needed to do before she took it.

She opened the bottom drawer of her dresser and took out a heavy length of chain with a steel clip attached to each end. Holding one end of the chain under her chin, she twined the other end around her wrist and clipped it firmly closed. Then she climbed onto her bed and clipped the other end of the chain around her bedpost.

And now for the pill, which was on her bedside table with the cup of water. When she'd swallowed it, Lila lay back on her pillow and waited to fall asleep.

Let the moon rise. It wasn't going to touch her tonight.

Perhaps it was the sleeping pill that gave Lila such a strange dream. Strange, and yet familiar. Almost everything she dreamed had actually happened to her before.

This was the dream: She was lying on her bed, sleeping, when she suddenly heard the motorcycle pulling up outside her house. She lay there motionless, praying that he would leave. But he wouldn't. The motorcycle idled gently outside her window for what seemed like hours.

Finally Lila slipped free of the chain around her

arm—it was easy to do in a dream, of course—and went to the window.

The boy was gazing up at her, and for once his expression was unguarded. She could read every emotion on his face. Love, and longing, and impatience that she was taking so long, yet the patience to wait for her forever if he had to—and the certainty that in the end she wouldn't be able to resist him. Lila had never seen someone's countenance say so much.

She could have stood there forever, reading his expressions, but he finally spoke.

"I know you know who I am," he said, holding her gaze. "You can't deny me. *And you can't deny yourself.*"

And with that, he transformed into . . .

"Of course," Lila whispered. "The wolf. *My* wolf. Why didn't I guess sooner?"

The boy on the motorcycle was the other werewolf.

It explained everything. Why he'd turned up when he had. Why she had recognized him in his wolf guise. Why Corey had become so meaningless so quickly.

The two of us belong together.

Hearing her thought, the other wolf raised his head and stared into her eyes. Instantly Lila, too, transformed. Without hesitation she sprang through the window and landed next to him.

The two wolves touched noses and began to run. But after the first step Lila fell headlong. She had forgotten the chain on her foreleg.

I have to catch up! she thought in a panic. The chain was cutting cruelly into her skin. Frantically she tried to gnaw it off, but even her wolf's teeth were useless against the cold iron.

Wait for me! she tried to call, but the other wolf was already too far away for her ever to reach him.

She stood, whining a little, and watched him until he became a dot in the moonlight. Then, heartbroken, she pointed her nose at the moon and began to howl.

The dream ended there.

When she woke up in the morning, Lila saw that her arm was still chained. But somehow, during the night, she had managed to snap off the bedpost like a matchstick.

The Boy

It is early evening, so early that the moon hasn't put in its appearance yet. The boy has parked his motorcycle. He is lying on his back in the woods, his leather jacket spread over him like a coat. It's very cold out, but he doesn't want to build a fire. Fires keep the animals away, and he likes their company. He stares up at the stars and tries to decide what to do next.

It is still too early to take her away, he thinks. She doesn't know enough about being a wolf yet. Besides, she's so young. A girl like that has always lived with a roof over her head and enough to eat. How will she cope in the wild? He thinks she can learn, but is it fair to take her when she's still so untested?

Still, this attack she made worries him. It suggests to him that she's more powerful than she realizes. If that's true, she won't be able to control herself. For her own safety, he should get her away where she can learn without all these human distractions.

The boy is used to sleeping on the ground, but he can't seem to get comfortable tonight. He tells himself that it's because he'll be transforming as soon as the moon rises high enough. But he suspects he's really worried about the girl.

At last he makes up his mind. He'll do it tomorrow.

Far, far away, on a hilltop, a hooded figure is staring into a meager fire. Once, he was the boy's guardian, not that the boy remembers the horrors of those years.

The hooded figure smiles. The two wolves will be together soon. He can feel it.

CHAPTER 16

When she looked back later, Lila was never able to remember how she had spent the days of her third full moon. Somehow she got herself up and dressed; locked the silent, empty house behind her; and managed to find her way to school. But what she said when her parents called home, how she got herself from class to class, whether she ate anything at all during that time, she never knew.

She did remember, though, that the boy on the motorcycle never showed up on the day after she had dreamed about him. When Lila awoke—the dream still burning in her mind, the snapped bed-post hanging strangely from her wrist—she raced to the window, sure he would actually be outside waiting for her.

He wasn't, and Lila burst into tears.

He wasn't there when she walked home from school, and she had purposely chosen the longest route home, hoping he would manage to find her.

He hadn't even driven by the house when it began to get dark. Inside the living room, Lila lay dejectedly on the sofa. She glanced at the clock every so often, shocked at how slowly time was passing. Every time a car went by, her heart lifted. Every time she realized it wasn't the motorcycle after all, she wished she were dead.

Even if Lila had remembered about locking herself in her room before the moon rose, she wouldn't have been able to get upstairs to do it. Depression had locked her to the sofa all by itself. This time she couldn't break free.

Until the doorbell rang. Lila jumped to her feet. *He's here! He's come to get me!* her heart caroled joyfully. She raced to the front door and hurled it open. Oh, all the waiting had been worth it now that he was finally—

It was like getting kicked in the stomach to realize who was actually at the door.

"Corey," Lila said flatly. "I wasn't expecting you."

Corey was standing out on the front porch with a curious expression of distaste on his face.

"That's fairly obvious," he said coldly. "Don't worry. I won't take up more of your time than I have to."

Before Lila could stop him, he had walked into the house. He knew the Crawfords' house very well, after all. He headed into the living room, plunked himself down in the wing chair by the fireplace, and turned to face Lila.

She was standing in the doorway, glaring at him. "Make yourself at home, why don't you?" she suggested icily.

"Don't start, Lila," Corey warned her. He had never spoken to her like that before. "Don't say anything until you hear what I've come for."

Wordless, Lila sank down onto the sofa and stared at him.

"Karin is begging to see you," Corey said.

She opened her mouth to object.

"Literally begging. I visit her every day. She'll never be any better, I don't think," Corey went on before she could speak. "And I want to know"—he took a deep breath—"I want to know what you did to her. Because Karin keeps going on and on with this horrible story, and it's all about you.''

So it was here at last. Corey was on her trail. Still, she'd better deny everything. She didn't know how much *he* knew.

"Corey, I don't know what you're talking—"

"I taped her," Corey interrupted curtly. "I thought that hearing her voice might convince you to help her. Since nothing *I've* said will do it."

He pulled a tape out of his pocket, walked over to the tape deck, and inserted the tape. Then he turned to Lila.

"For the record," he said, "I still love you."

He punched the start button. Karin's voice filled the living room.

Only it wasn't Karin's voice. At least, it was nothing like the voice Lila knew. It was a shrill, broken monotone that hardly sounded human.

"*Please* don't let her, *please* don't let her—Lila, what are you doing? What's happening to you?" The voice rose to a scream. "*No! No! Get it away from me!*

"Those teeth," the voice babbled on. "Teeth. Sharp. Her face. Where's Lila's *face*? Not claws! Oh,

God, I'm so sorry! Please don't let her, please no, please *no!*"

Now they could hear the soothing tones of an older woman, a nurse, perhaps. But Karin wouldn't quiet down. She gave a low, hoarse, hacking cough. It sounded more like an old man's than a young girl's. Then she went on ranting.

"Get up, Lila! Why can't you stand up? Stand up and—oh, my God, I'm so sorry! You've got to believe me! I'll never do it. Not my throat, Lila! Please not my throat! She's going to rip it out!"

Lila covered her ears, but she couldn't shut out the dreadful sound of that voice.

"Blood," Karin whimpered. Again she coughed hoarsely. "So much blood. All over me. She did it because I . . . I'm going to die. Out here. I know. No one to—She did it. She did it." The voice was rising rapidly, and speeding up. "She's coming back for me, I know it. Don't let her come back! *Don't let her*—"

And the words dissolved into a fit of hideous screaming.

Corey switched off the tape.

The silence was thick with accusation.

Finally he cleared his throat. "Of course I know she's imagining things," he said. "But Lila, what did you *do* to her to make her imagine those things? For God's sake, you've got to tell me! I won't hurt you. I won't do anything to you. I only want to know the truth." His voice cracked. "Please," he said.

A thin beam of moonlight began to filter its way through one of the windows.

For a second Lila stared down at her hands. Then she lifted her head and stared into Corey's eyes.

"All right," she said quietly. "You wanted the truth, and I'll give it to you. I guess it doesn't matter who knows, really."

The moonlight was brighter now, and higher in the window, but Lila didn't see it. "Corey, something has happened to me," she started again. "I don't expect you to believe me. But a couple of months ago, I—"

At that moment the beam of moonlight, now even higher in the window, moved gently across her eyes.

So gently, to cause such a reaction. The transformation began to explode inside her.

"No! I can't be here when it happens," Lila cried in a panic.

"When what happens? What do you mean?" Corey asked, bewildered.

Lila was on her feet now. She couldn't stay in this room. Not because she was afraid of having Corey see her, or not only that.

If I stay here, I won't be able to help killing him. And I can't let myself do that.

It was almost her last thought as a human. She knocked Corey down in her haste to get across the living room. Frantically she beat on the glass of the nearest window. It wouldn't break. The transformation already beginning, Lila gathered all her strength and dove through the window headfirst.

"Lila!" Corey called after her. "Lila, come back!"

But Lila was picking herself off the ground and racing away toward the forest. Shards of glass showered from her body as she ran.

And as she runs, she drops to all fours. She feels her bones beginning to lengthen, her hands turning to paws, her jaw stretching out. How welcome this change is, at last. There was no reason to fight it, was there? After all, it is what she has always been meant for.

"You can't deny yourself," the boy in her dream said. Now she knows he was right. To deny herself would be to shut out this essential part of her nature. And to do that would kill her.

She knows where to find him. They haven't had much time together yet, but she's certain he'll be there.

He is waiting for her at the edge of the forest. Motionless, as always, his black fur shining in the light of the full moon.

When she reaches him, there are tears in his eyes. But of course, being a wolf, she doesn't know what they are. And of course, being so new to emotion, he doesn't either.

CHAPTER 17

Sun streamed into Lila's bedroom, filling it with warmth and light. It was almost eight o'clock in the morning, and she was still in bed. She had decided not to go to school today after all.

Why bother? She was leaving home today.

There was no reason to stay any longer. She was in too much danger here. Besides, she had reached the point where nothing in the life she'd been living meant anything to her. This life wasn't reality anymore. Reality was out in the wild now.

This was the last time Lila would ever sleep in her bed. The last time, perhaps, that she'd ever get to sleep late. She might as well make the most of it.

She stretched luxuriously and looked around her room. She would never see it again, but she felt strangely unbothered by the thought.

Her parents—should she feel sorry about leaving them? Try as she might, Lila couldn't manage to squeeze out much guilt. Anyway, life would go much more smoothly for them once she was out of their way.

I wonder if they'll call the police again. Maybe they'll just let it go.

Actually, there was almost no one she'd miss anymore. Except, possibly, Corey. Once in a while, maybe, she'd think fondly of him.

Thinking about Corey now, Lila frowned slightly. How much of the truth had he guessed—or seen? He might turn out to be dangerous if he knew too much. But of course there was no way to know that. She just hated leaving a loose end. . . .

Half an hour later, Lila, now dressed in a sweater and jeans, was brushing out her just-washed hair. When she finished, she put down the brush and stared at herself in the mirror for a long time.

Who knows what I'll look like the next time I see myself in a mirror?

She walked through the house quickly, saying good-bye to every room. She was relieved to see that nothing tugged at her emotions. None of her possessions cried out to come along with her. Everything seemed perfectly content to stay where it was.

At the desk in the hallway, Lila paused for a minute.

"Should I write a note?" she murmured aloud.

She tapped her fingers across the top of the desk, thinking. No, she decided. What could she possibly say that would make sense to her parents? She didn't even know where she was going!

All right, no note. Then it was really time to go.

Lila let herself out of the house, locked the door, and put the key into the mailbox. Her parents would find it there.

What a beautiful fall day it was, just right for a trip.

Lila smiled up at the sky and headed down the street.

She had only gone a few steps when she heard the roar of a motorcycle behind her. When it caught up to her, she climbed aboard and put her arms around the driver's waist.

In seconds the two of them had disappeared from view.

EPILOGUE

Two wolves race silently through the wintry dark and vanish on the horizon, their pace perfectly matched. They are miles from any human dwellings. No one is there to see them.

It is the last night of the full moon.

Ann Hodgman has written over forty books. She lives in Washington, Connecticut, with her husband and two children.

*A wild and dangerous love is only as far
away as the next full moon . . .*

Ann Hodgman's stunning new Children of the
Night series continues with

DARK
MUSIC

The only thing Lila knows about the bewitchingly handsome Rider is that he's a werewolf like herself. Now this
mysterious stranger is Lila's sole companion on a desperate flight from the hometown and everyday life she's
been forced to leave behind. But who exactly is Rider
and what does he want from Lila? The full moon brings
them together, but daylight brings only uncertainty and
misunderstanding. While Lila finds Rider impenetrable
in his brooding silence, she has no choice but to stay
with him. Only together can they hope to win against the
powerful forces that are pursuing them relentlessly—no
matter how far or how fast they run.

Available in February, 1994 U.S. $3.50/Can. $4.50
ISBN 0-14-036375-0

Special bonus chapter from *DARK MUSIC*,
the tantalizing sequel to *DARK DREAMS*,
available in February 1994 from High Flyer™

CHAPTER ONE

*It is the first night of the full moon. The blue-white landscape
lies before them like a gift waiting to be ripped open.*

*The huge black wolf is the male, his smaller, paler compan-
ion, the female. They have waited so long to be together.*

*The two wolves have only been aware of each other for a few
weeks. Yet, on some deep level, they have known each other
forever. Already they share so much. From their first meeting,
they have been able to communicate—wordlessly, yet perfectly
clearly.*

*Once in a while the female pauses uncertainly. She hasn't
been a wolf for as long as the male has.*

You're sure it's all right? No one will catch us?

We're safe now, *the male assures her.*

And we'll always be together? *she asks him.*

Always.

For their human counterparts, it will not be so easy.

*He had told her his name was Rider. And that was practi-
cally the only thing he had told her. In the weeks and days*

they'd been traveling together, all Lila had really learned about him was his name.

"Rider?" she had asked on the first day of their journey together. "What kind of name is that?"

"A name," he'd answered uncomfortably, glancing at his motorcycle. It was parked beside the campfire like a third person.

Lila thought she was beginning to understand. "It's not the name your parents gave you, is it?" she said slowly. "It's what you call yourself. It's what you do," she finished, staring at the bike.

"I don't remember my parents," he told her simply. "Rider is the only name I have."

Rider is the only name I have . . .

What kind of person was it that Lila'd given up everything for—her home, her friends, her boyfriend, her whole life? She had walked out of her parents' house, climbed onto Rider's motorcycle, and driven away. Thrown out everything familiar as easily as if she were throwing away a scrap of paper.

A crow called hoarsely to its companion in the woods. As if the sound had been their alarm clock, one drowsy bird began to chirp, then another.

Shivering a little, Lila quietly raised herself up on one elbow and looked over at the boy sleeping on the ground nearby. They had arrived late the night before and set up camp in a little glade they'd found in the woods—a pretty spot, now drenched in cold dew.

A chilly dawn light was breaking, but Rider was sound asleep on the rocky ground. He could sleep anywhere, Lila had learned, anywhere they could park the motorcycle. He just put his head down, and he was out. Lila, on the other hand, had trouble getting used to sleeping outdoors. She missed her mattress and pillow. It was one more difference between them.

How strange that you could feel such a deep connection to someone and yet not know him at all. You could spend all your time thinking about him. You could sleep next to him every night and wake up with him every day. And still have no idea what he was like.

In all the stories where the young couple rode off into the sunset together, no one ever talked about what happened later, how they learned to get along. . . .

He's so good-looking, though, *Lila mused as she stared at Rider now. As always, looking at him made her a little dizzy. His mouth was faintly scowling, his slanting eyebrows were drawn together in a frown as though a dream was troubling him. His long black hair, sleep-tousled, almost covered his face. Lila wished she dared reach over and brush it aside. But somehow she was afraid to touch him.*

Not that I don't want to, *Lila thought ruefully. But the time was never right. They were too unaccustomed to each other. There were still so many rules to work out between them—*

Without warning, Rider opened his eyes and stared straight into hers.

"*Good morning,*" *Lila stammered. For some reason it embarrassed her to have him think she'd been watching him sleep.*

Instantly awake, as always, he sat up and stretched. "How's the fire?" he asked.

Lila's heart sank. Living this long in the wild with Rider should have taught her one thing. Thinking about survival was the single imperative. It was something Lila was woefully unused to doing.

"*I—I'm sorry,*" *she faltered. "I haven't checked it yet."*

Rider said nothing. A few long strides and he was at the remains of their campfire. Silently, he bent and scrabbled for nearby leaves and twigs to rekindle the blaze as he blew steadily on the dying embers.

Lila couldn't see his eyes, yet felt their silent accusation. Angry at her own failure, she lashed out. "So what if the stupid fire goes out?" she raged. "Big deal! We have matches. We can always relight it, can't we?"

Rider looked up. His steady gaze pinned Lila as he spoke. "We don't have many matches left," he began.

"*We can always buy more,*" *Lila blurted.*

"*Lila.*" *Rider rarely spoke her name. As he did now, Lila felt the frisson that took her away with him, that kept her with* him. "We can't go into stores and towns unless we absolutely have to," Rider continued evenly. "We can't give anyone any clues about where you are. Besides, we have a long way to go, and we need to save our money as long as we can." He took a deep breath when he'd finished. This was the longest speech Lila'd heard him make in all their time together.

"That's one thing I've been meaning to ask you," Lila suddenly said. "Where are we going? Why won't you—"

"Anyway," Rider interrupted, "it's safer for us if the fire goes all night. Keeps the wild animals away."

At that, Lila couldn't help grinning. "And God knows we need to keep the wild animals away," she said ironically.

An unwilling smile tugged at Rider's mouth, too. Almost as if he didn't realize what he was doing, he reached out and touched Lila's cheek for a second. Then he quickly turned back to the fire.

Where are they going? Only one person knows that.

That person lives alone, far from Rider and Lila, in a stone house that looks as though it hasn't been touched in five hundred years. Surrounded by dark, looming pines, the house at first might look to a visitor like a fairy-tale cottage. Then the visitor would notice that the ground outside the cottage door was strewn with bones, that the garden lining the wall was filled with dark, spiky, ill-smelling plants that could not possibly be flowers, and that the cottage's small leaded windows were utterly impenetrable to light.

At that point, the visitor might begin to realize that the house really looked more like a fairy-tale witch's den than a cozy little cottage. Hastily he would back away down the winding path he'd followed there, shuddering with relief at his narrow escape.

In any case, no visitor would ever venture deep enough into the woods to find this little house. But inside it lives the person who holds Rider's and Lila's destinies in his wicked hand.

He is there now—a man as ancient as he is evil. He's staring down at a thick stone table as though the tracings in the stone held a message for him. Suddenly he bends down to the hearth and picks up a handful of ashes. He scatters them over the table's surface, lets them settle, and then reads the pattern they leave.

What he sees makes him frown. With a sweep of his arm, he scatters the ashes and takes an animal skull off a dusty shelf next to him. It is filled with a blood-red liquid.

He holds the skull high above his head, then lets a spurt of liquid splash onto the table. It hits the stone surface with a hiss, seething and bubbling for a few seconds before it settles into a clotted stain.

This new message is more pleasing. Smiling grimly, he traces a path through the rusty ooze with a gnarled forefinger. Now he is certain his directions will be followed.

Then he tips his head back and drinks the rest of the liquid from the skull.

A visitor, looking closely, might mistake this skull for a

dog's. But no dog was ever this big. No dog ever had teeth this long or this sharp.

"Get up, Lila."

It was Rider's voice, and it reached Lila through the pitch dark of a sound sleep.

"What?" she said groggily. "Why?"

"We have to go," Rider answered. "Right now."

Lila opened her eyes, hoping there had been some kind of mistake. But no, it was obviously the middle of the night, and Rider was standing in front of her fully dressed. His sleeping bag was neatly rolled up behind him. The dying campfire gave the only light.

"It's too cold," Lila moaned, burrowing deeper down into her own sleeping bag. "We just got here."

"We're changing course." Rider's voice was clipped.

"In the middle of the night?" Suddenly wide awake, Lila scrambled out of her sleeping bag. "Did you hear something? Is someone looking for us?" she asked quickly.

"We have to take a different route. We have to go north."

"What do you mean, have to? Why?" Lila said blankly.

"We don't have a choice, Lila. We're stuck together." His hands were gripping her shoulders painfully. "And . . . we can't get out of this."

He lowered his face until it was almost touching hers. Both of them were breathing hard now.

For a long, long moment they stared at each other.

THE DARK CARD

BY AMY EHRLICH

Laura thinks she's playing to win . . .
but at what cost?

Laura loves the flashiness and glamour of the casinos. When she sits at the blackjack table, dressed in silken clothes and beautiful jewelry, she feels like a sophisticated woman of the world. But Laura is living a double life, and it's about to catch up with her.

ISBN 014-036332-7